THE CLUB

LADIES LOVE IT!

RICHARD LEE

*Dedicated to a world in need of
love and imagination.*

"Ten men waiting for me at the door? Send one of them home, I'm tired."
- Mae West

CONTENTS

FOREWORD

The EROS CRESCENT novels take you on a journey like no other - to places you couldn't imagine - a female friendly sex club or a privately owned members-only dogging venue; the toy-boy life of a writer working on the Amalfi coast and much much more. *THE CLUB* and the other novellas - *JESSICA, MARIA, HELEN, MARY, ALICE* and *JANICE* - are extracts taken from *The Fifi Code, Eros Crescent* and *Mount Eros*.

PREFACE

"It's basically a sex club. It shows end-to-end blue movies for the six hours it is open on six days of the week. But before you say that it sounds sordid or creepy, I should tell you more about it."
    —*from Mount Eros*

MARIA TELLS ROGER

IT WAS Maria's cleaning day and Roger made sure he was up and shaved and dressed and presentable before heading downstairs for his first coffee of the day.

As usual, Maria was looking attractive and Roger appreciated both her looks and her energy.

For the umpteenth time, Roger thought about if and when he would make it known to Maria that he knew about her secret Tuesday morning visits to his bed when he was in a deep sleep and how much he enjoyed her gentle sucking his cock before exiting, well before he awoke.

With Caroline in London, now was probably a good time to do it and even perhaps move things along even further and seduce the woman. He was ready to confront Maria but when he said her name as she folded clean tea towels on the kitchen table, Maria got in first.

"Roger, I have one thing to tell you and one thing to ask you. Is now a good time?"

Maria's smile was irresistible and Roger indicated that he wanted to hear what she wanted to tell him. He assumed that they would be about the house and working. He was in for a shock.

"Please! No time like the present as they say in cheap novels."

Maria fixed him with a look that foretold that a secret was about to be divulged.

"As you know, I do housework and sometimes cooking for a number of wealthy clients here in the Western suburbs. One of my customers is a woman named Desley who is the daughter of the long dead but well known brothel keeper, Kathleen Mary Leigh. Kathleen Leigh famously bought the house near by and she was instrumental in naming this crescent Eros Crescent. Mount Eros is the name of their house; number thirteen, on the other side of the track leading up the mountain."

Roger smiled and said how he knew the name and had read the inscription on the plaque at the edge of the park.

"Well, a couple of months ago, Desley opened a club. She runs a charity for older and out of work prostitutes, so she thought what better way to raise money than exploiting an activity she knows a lot about. She has slowly built the reputation of the club so that now it is so popular, she has been forced to limit membership and stop accepting new enrolments, unless of course, another member leaves. But she now has plans to open a second club on the other side of the harbour, probably at Neutral Bay or somewhere on that side of the bridge, anyway."

Roger put up his hand.

"Before you go on, Maria, just fill me in on what is special about The Club?"

Maria laughed and for a moment Roger thought he saw her blush.

"It's basically a sex club. It shows end-to-end blue movies for the six hours it is open on six days of the week. But before you say that it sounds sordid or creepy, I should tell you more about it.

"Desley went to a lot of effort to set the place up. It is beautifully designed and very functional. But what makes it unique is that it is female friendly. She thinks it is the first of its kind and she thinks she will eventually be able to sell the concept around the world.

This leads me to why I'm telling you about it. Desley is looking for a person to write up the story of The Club and what she has achieved. She wants something in print that properly describes the club, the way it functions and how it is used. She also wants something that can be used as a prospectus for likely overseas clients.

I told her that I thought I knew someone who would be good for the job and who might be interested. I lent her a copy of your previous book and she loved it and enthusiastically said she wanted to meet you.

Roger looked at Maria intently, digesting what she was telling him. His first reaction was of disbelief that such a place could exist.

"I've visited sex shop movie theatres in New York and in Amsterdam. I can't see how they could possibly be restructured to provide enticing entertainment for anyone other than the most desperate people, mostly male and very rarely, female.

Have you been to the club Maria? And if so, what was it like? From a woman's point of view."

Roger watched as Maria coloured up again.

"Well, yes I have, Roger. I have long enjoyed an active sex life, both with men and with women and Desley knows that. Desley gave me a free membership to The Club and I can only report that so far, I've loved it. It does it for me and from what I observe, it does it for all the other women I see there. And the men seem very happy too."

Roger was in a sort of shock. The sad pervy men attempting to grope the unattractive and equally sad women who he had observed in adult theatres overseas could never fit with what Maria was telling him.

"Desley said she would be happy to pay a considerable sum of money for the story and hoped I would be able to interest you in the project.

"There is one other thing though, before you meet her. I am allowed to take a visitor to the club. It's all part of the membership. Three visitor tickets a year. She insists that I take you along to see the place working prior to her meeting you. She acknowledges that, having had that experience, you might not want to take on the job. I think she is right. You need to see it working.

"I suggest we go early one afternoon. You can accompany me and meet my friend Veronica. We mostly sit together. Then you can wander off and explore the club and we can see each other back here if we don't catch up at The Club at the end of the day. How does that sound, Roger?"

Roger was thinking fast. His natural interest in human behaviour was being teased out in a way that was hard to switch off. There was also an erotic component that could not be ignored. But his answer was swift.

"How could I not want to take up your offer, Maria? You might or might not have noticed that I have always acted appropriately in your company but I should put you on notice that this could change the instant we arrive at the club."

Maria laughed sympathetically and stared at him defiantly.

"Why would you wait until you were somewhere where there was likely to be stiff opposition, Roger? But perhaps a visit to The Club will encourage inappropriate behaviour in the future. We'll see."

Roger was immediately excited by Maria's suggestive stance. But he had questions.

"Maria? What would you say was the thing that made The Club experience so appealing to women? I can easily understand men being drawn towards interactions with women but I really do want to know what is the appeal for the ladies?"

Suddenly, Maria took on a different persona, showing an intellectual interest in what I had asked her.

"I'd put uncertainty and anticipation at the head of the list. The uncertainty coupled with the expectation and excitement of receiving unsolicited sexual attention, i.e., "Will someone I do not know, try to do something sexual to me when I wasn't expecting it?"

"The second thing, strangely enough, is the feeling of empowerment. A woman at The Club knows that ultimately she is safe but like all good stories, the opportunity is offered whereby the woman can suspend disbelief. She can pretend for just a short time, pretend that she will be surprised by titillating things that might happen to her, sexual things that she does not normally experience in her daily life.

"And thirdly, wanting to be adored is a natural trait of all women, even if it might be only temporarily. How much a man adores her is demonstrated by his persistence in wooing her despite the difficulties she might put in his way. She is in a position to reward or reject her would-be lover; or most likely, tease him and enjoy his tortured persistence.

"I love to have my boobs displayed and played with, but a man must work hard to persuade me before his fingers touch my nipples."

Roger eyed Maria and her bust, with more than intellectual appreciation.

"Tell me where to meet you and when, Maria, and I'll be there."

Maria smiled a wicked and beautiful smile. Then she reached forward and her hand closed over the bulge in Roger's pants. With her other hand, she unbuttoned her blouse exposing a low-cut bra.

"Bare my breasts Roger, please. I don't want to wait any longer. We've waited too long already."

A beautiful breast in each hand and a willing woman on the end of his penis while her legs waved wildly in the air, cleared all thoughts of anything else from Roger's head and he melted into the moment and between Maria's thighs.

This had been a long-time coming, and yes, he would tell Caroline, eventually.

INTRODUCTION TO THE CLUB

ROGER WAS VERY SURPRISED to discover the location of The Club. Only a short walk from his own house and he'd never suspected that it was there.

He met Maria in what was originally intended as a car park, many years back, but which was now just a large flattened expanse of land that lay at the foot of the mount and stretched behind both numbers thirteen and eleven Eros Crescent.

Marie looked extraordinary. She was not wearing her usual black skirt and top but instead, a very short red miniskirt and a light cream coloured blouse with a frilly low neckline. Her bright red lipstick and her red high heels and white stockings pushed her appearance over the top. She took his hand and looked into Roger's eyes.

"Sorry about this outfit Roger, but it is the second Tuesday of the month. It's when Veronica and I meet two older lesbian ladies who we both happen to work for. They are super rich and live in big houses next door to each other in Vaucluse. They love to come over here once a month and have us together and wanting us to look as slutty as we can make ourselves without getting arrested. Interestingly, of the things that some women regret not doing in their younger days, dressing as sluts is one of them, although they will never admit it. If you sat close by and watched, you would be amazed at how many women approach us when we look like this. Far more interest from women than men."

Roger thanked Maria for her explanation saying that he was a little taken aback when he first saw her.

"I do hope today is going to work for you Roger. And can I say quickly, that when you wander off to see the sights, feel free to come back to me if I'm around. I will always be more than willing to bare myself to you. And Vickie will want you as well, I know what she likes. Mind you, though. today we might look just bit too slutty for your more refined taste."

Roger laughed and took Marie's hand and squeezed it.

"I just hope I can make myself ignore you both. Just for research purposes of course."

Marie burst out laughing.

"Now while I'm thinking about it, tell me about the films, Maria. The few I've seen in porn cinemas were often violent. How are the films here selected."

"Oh yes! I was going to mention that and then forgot. Desley's brother, Arnold has worked in the sex industry all his working life and is an authority on blue movies. He has selected an extensive range for viewing at the Club and all of them he and his sister have judged as female friendly or at least, close to. No rape or violence apart from the occasional bit of slap and tickle. The female club members seem to love them and can happily just sit and watch a movie with their skirts pulled up and their legs apart and their fingers busy. Seeing and watching them playing with themselves is one of the little known delights of being a member.

Alvie at the front desk even has a list of favourite movies that women clients would like to view again. Interestingly, the number one favourite is called Debt Collectors and depicts a woman being told by three gangsters that because her husband can't pay his debts, she will have to pay them for him, in kind. You can imagine what follows."

Roger stopped walking and took hold of the beautiful Maria and kissed her. When he thought he should stop, she wouldn't let him go and pressed her hand on his crotch.

"So looking this slutty hasn't put you off Roger. You must promise me that you will act inappropriately at your house whenever the idea enters your head. I will love it."

They were inside the door now and Roger looked around.

At reception, Maria flashed her membership card on the electronic reader and pointed to Roger.

"My guest, Alvie."

The older woman looked at Roger and smiled.

Alvie reached over and fastened a small tag to Roger's shirt showing the number 28.

"This must be your first visit? Haven't noticed you here before."

For just a moment, Roger felt like a naughty boy who'd been caught looking at a copy of a lad magazine.

"Yes! I'm looking forward to it."

"I'm sure you will enjoy yourself, love. Just remember the first rule, Slow and Gentle. That way no woman will ever disappoint you."

Maria beamed at Alvie and then at Roger.

"Let me know if you want to practice either or both of those things, Roger. Happy to give you a lesson if you think you need it."

Roger and Alvie laughed, enjoying Maria's innuendo. Alvie handed Roger a brochure entitled The Club Rules: Advice for New Members.

"Just in case you enjoy yourself so much that you decide to put your name down for membership, Roger.

ROGER ON OFFER

ROGER WAS IMPRESSED from the very beginning. The Club entrance area was bright and airy with white walls and brightly coloured doors and woodwork, and signage was clear and tasteful.

A small counter offered peppermints and jelly beans and chocolate almonds along with condoms and wet wipes, and lubricants in a range of perfumed and non perfumed products in squeegee bottles.

This small foyer area which led to the entrance to the cinema, was flanked by male and female bathrooms on either side, and signs pointed the way to two other venues. Signposts pointed to the Home Deliveries room and to Gals Only, and The Parlour seemed self-evident. Well, sort of. Roger had no trouble guessing the purpose of the Gals Only room but the Home Deliveries did not translate into something he could immediately identify and The Parlour, well that could be anything.

"Ready, Roger?"

Roger looked at Maria and smiled.

"Definitely ready, Maria."

It took only a few moments for Roger's eyes to adjust to the dim theatre lighting provided by the cinema screen. A movie played and provided gentle narration of a sexual encounter and with the voice of a woman screaming yes, yes, in the background.

The floor sloped down quite significantly allowing easy viewing over other patrons heads.

As he slowly adjusted his eyes to the dim light and took in the scene, Roger was again impressed by the design and layout. Each row of wide, red vinyl covered seats, contained four sets of four seats leaving a wider access aisle up the middle as well as those on either side. He counted twelve rows. There was a wide walkway at the very back where people could stand or another row of seating could be installed. Another wide walkway divided the front three rows from the rest. A quick calculation showed that the theatre could seat one hundred and ninety patrons.

People were scattered around the theatre, some alone, some as couples and there was at least two sets of three people.

Maria pointed out to him that that the three front rows were off limits to men unless they were with a consenting female partner. These front rows catered for couples and women on their own who did not want to be approached by other members.

Lone women would go there to simply watch the movie and likely touch themselves if so inclined. Occassionally - according to Maria - two women in a row might exchange glances and indicate that they would be happy to enjoy the other's company for mutual touching and kissing in which case, one or the other would get up and move next to her newly found friend.

Maria took Roger's hand and led him along one side to a row half-way down. Then she whispered, "Veronica will find us when she gets here shortly."

On the screen, two women were now laying on a bed kissing, each fully clothed but obviously interested in slowly removing bits of the others apparel. Close by, a semi-clothed man sat exposing himself on the bed and holding himself at the ready, awaiting the call.

Maria took Rogers hand and lent towards him and whispered. "Once your eyes have adjusted, feel free to wander off and check every-thing. I would suggest you start at the back wall where most men hang around while working out their next move and who they might approach. Your learning starts now, Roger. Best of luck."

Roger gave Maria a peck on the cheek then rose and turned to walk to the back. But he couldn't help noticing a woman two rows back. She was not alone. She stared straight ahead, stoney faced and completely absorbed in the movie, seemingly oblivious to the two men who sat either side of her gently groping her fully exposed, neat womanly breasts.

But then Roger saw that wasn't all that was going on. The woman had an arm stretched out on either side of her with each hand holding and slowly rubbing a man's fully erect cock. This was bordering on the erotic existential moments of 1920s Paris and Berlin that Roger had studies some years ago. He wanted to stop and watch but thought it would be rude to be a gawker, and moved on.

Roger couldn't help but wonder what was going on in the woman's head. Was she excited? Was she getting what she came for? Then he remembered Maria's explanation: "She can pretend for just a short time, pretend that she will be surprised by titillating things that might happen to her, sexual things that she does not normally experience in her daily life."

So this really is a properly functioning porn cinema, Roger murmured to himself.

Sometimes in life, things happen really quickly, no matter how prepared you thought you were for sudden shocks.

An arm shot out and grabbed Roger's arm and suddenly a tall thin elegant woman was by his side.

"We are just what you are looking for, darling."

The woman dragged Roger in to where she was sitting alongside her more substantially built lady friend. Before he could say a word, the woman put her hand behind his head and dragged it down between her companions large stocking-clad thighs and ordered him to "lick my friends pussy." But she didn't stop there. As Roger's face drowned in a beautiful tangle of wet and perfumed pubic hair, he felt his trousers being removed and suddenly his member was first in the hands of the thin lady and then in her mouth.

But then Roger had an epiphany. It was an extraordinary moment. He was transported to a time when he was sixteen-year-old and on holidays at his aunt Ella's sheep property.

There was a moment during the dinner commemorating his late uncles birthday, when the slightly tipsy Ella had asked Roger to get down under the dinner table and retrieve her serviette. It was there that he had discovered a pair of magnificent stockinged legs spread wide apart and, due to the randy aunt's lack of knickers, Roger found himself looking at a very large hairy pussy while in the background he heard his aunt call out, "take your time darling, have whatever you want."

But the epiphany didn't stop there. Aunt Ella's housekeeper, the thin and delightful Sheila, when later helping Roger get his now fully inebriated aunt to bed, had looked into his eyes then grabbed him and removed his trousers and her own clothing and dragged him down onto the bed beside his now sleeping aunt. Then she provided him with such a fucking as had not been matched since that day. This memory of his first sexual experience had propelled him forward in life to a rich and energetic love life. That first encounter with raw woman-hood helped add sensual substance to both his personal life and to his work as a writer.

Roger now found himself again in that moment. The thin lady who had grabbed him and removed his trousers now hung onto his cock with her mouth as though she wanted to become a part of him, just as Sheila had done all those years ago. And the aunt Ella lady was squirming beneath his cunnilingus assault on her giant vagina.

At an appropriate moment, Roger chanced a glance upwards to see what was happing topside.

The view was erotic to say the least. Two fully exposed mammoth white mammaries floated on a body that laid back in the seat. The woman's head was pushed over the back of the seat by a hand on her neck. A mouth sucked a breast and Rogers proxy aunt Ella was taking turns at sucking the two cocks being offered by men standing on either side of her head and behind her. But Roger's efforts won the day and the big lady threw up her body and came with a violent scream before pulling Roger's head further in between her legs.

Now it was the thin ladies turn and she wasn't going to miss out.

Dragging Roger's head from between her friends legs she stared into the darkness where she thought his eyes were.

"Give me what you gave her, you beautiful man."

Suddenly the lady was laying flat on the floor with her legs waving in the air and wide apart and a hand held Roger's face against her comparatively tiny wet pussy.

Roger didn't hesitate, moving straight into a repeat of the professional cunnilingus mode he had learnt from the lovely Italian ladies in Positano.

When the skinny Sheila substitute lady arched her back and screamed, Roger moved forward and plunged his cock into her willing wet vagina. She screamed again and bit him fiercely on his chest.

"Stay in me, lovely man. I'm coming again."

Roger rewarded her and himself by pushing in even harder. Then he exercised his preferred penis move, one taught him by those same experienced older ladies on the Amalfi coast. He pushed in hard, then, when the root end of his member was hard up against the woman's pelvic bone, Roger maintained the pressure against her clitoral area so that she could not move away from him. The effect was dramatic. The woman screamed once and came and then screamed again and came again and kept on repeating the happy event.

Roger knew that by not letting her back away, she would probably just keep orgasming again and again until she pleaded with him to stop. But the lovely lady couldn't bring herself to give up the magic of what Roger's cock was providing. In the end, she just stopped moving her body and began to sob. Only then did he pull back. He touched her face gently and cupped her mouth in his hand and kissed her. The effect was that she orgasmed once again. Then she slumped into a sleeping position and gently moaned.

The multiple cock sucking Ella lady above him suddenly came to life again and Roger felt a hand trying to pull him up by his shirt collar.

"Am I too late for some more?" came the voice of aunt Ella's double.

"Yes, you are," answered a dozy voice. "Sorry about that, darling, but we can find him again. He is a visitor and I've noted his visitor number. I think the club should offer him free membership. Never had anything like this before."

4

THE CLUB RULES

WHEN MARIA CALLED on Roger the morning after their visit to the Club, she announced that she had both bad news and some good news.

"Desley is away, overseas for three weeks, unfortunately, so she won't be able to see you yet."

Roger looked at Maria in her regular black outfit and found it difficult to remember her as the slut who took him to The Club the day before.

"And the good news?"

Maria bathed Roger with her most radiant smile.

"I can take you to the club again, but only if you want to go, Roger. I heard you had a good time with the lady mayor and her assistant. At least, they had a good time with you, or so the rumour goes."

Roger's face took on the amazed look of someone being told an impossible tale.

"They did? I didn't know who they were. Which one was the mayor? Oh, but no! Don't tell me. Better I don't know in case I meet either of them socially one day."

Now Maria couldn't believe what she was hearing.

"You didn't know who it was? I suppose that's possible. If you didn't already know them and it was your first visit to the Club. How funny is that? I can't wait to tell Veronica. She'll become hysterical and start rubbing herself. I can see her now."

Roger was thinking through the various scenarios that tried to answer the questions flooding into his brain. What was the Mayoress doing there anyway?

"Charlotte O'Connor has been a member of the club from the very beginning, as have a number of city councillors. It has been very good for Desley's project, helping her get through the various planning permissions and red tape and so on.

"So, are you up for another visit, Roger."

Roger was still busy thinking through his epiphany moments of yesterday, when vivid memories of his first ever sexual experiences had suddenly come to the fore and expressed themselves vividly when he made love with the two ladies. Surely that was a one-off event. He couldn't count on an epiphany event each time he fronted up to a lady. Maybe he just wasn't cut out for The Club. But then he remembered something he wanted to ask Maria about.

"Maria? I noticed a blond woman yesterday at the club. She was sitting alone down at the front. From my brief observations, she stayed on her own for the whole time. Don't suppose you know anything about her?"

Roger's brain had moved on, seduced by the image of the solitary female who had caught his eye. In truth, for some reason she reminded him of Agnes, his librarian lover he'd met at a book signing at Selfridges, many years back. Well dressed and demure. And those horn rimmed glasses helped too.

"Oh, Roger, you are funny. Yes, I do know who you mean. That was Yvette. It is well known that she has never been seen interacting with anyone at the club, male or female. In fact she never even talks to people there. Rumour has it that she is highly intelligent and an academic who, at a party a few years back was attracted to a man and ended up in bed with him and immediately fell pregnant. It turned out that the man was gay and this was really an accident from his point of view, and there was no way that he would enter into a relationship.

Roger raised his hand.

"Stop there, Maria. How do you know all this given that you have already said that Yvette is not forthcoming with any conversation. This must all surely be rumour and I'm a little suspicious of rumour. Enlighten me, please."

"Well, Roger, you already know that I do house work for a number of wealthy women. One of them knows Yvette and her parents so she is my prime source of information. Yvette lives with her three-year-old daughter in her parents house in Vaucluse. The parents and a housekeeper look after the child while Yvette is at work at Sydney University. I think I even know what faculty she's in. English Literature, I think. Don't know how I know that. I think that is what it is.

"So Roger, will you be my guest again at The Club? I'm sure there is still a lot there for you to learn about before you get to meet Desley. Do you have any questions at all? Now is the time to ask."

Roger already knew his answer.

"Yes, Maria, I would love to be your guest again and yes I have a couple of questions. Well, probably a lot of questions but most can wait.

"The first one is probably obvious but I don't get it. What happens in the room labelled Home Deliveries. There are three doors, each named after a plant or flower, I think, but they were all locked. What happens in those rooms, Maria."

Maria's face looked a bit sheepish and she seemed uncertain how to answer, staring up to the ceiling while she formulated a reply.

"Ok! More and more of the female members are using the Home Deliveries booths although a number of members still don't really approve of it. There is a sort of stigma attached to the concept. It's seen by those members who consider themselves more superior, as a British working-class activity which is beyond the pale.

Others have got over the shock and even if they don't yet use the rooms, they can appreciate the activity for those in need of it. By the way, those three booths are each named after a flower, Tulip, Buttercup and Primrose."

"Christ, Maria,for God's sake tell me what happens in the rooms. The suspense is driving me mad."

Maria giggled like a schoolgirl.

"Well, have you heard of dogging, Roger?"

Roger's mind took a sharp about face to accomodate what Maria had just said. Yes, he had heard of dogging.

"Are you serious, Maria? Do some members actually participate in this behaviour?"

"Oh yes, Roger, only the female members initiate it of course. But at the club, the activity is very different and we would never use the term dogging.

"Many women share the fantasy of being made love to - fucked, I suppose I should say - by more than one lover at the one time. The difference here is that the male suiters are club members and therefore "approved and certified" so to speak; not a load of stray smelly pervy types normally associated with dogging overseas.

"Not everyone uses the rooms, but more are enjoying it and dare I say that I can sort of understand why. We could perhaps discuss this at another time. Even I am a bit embarrassed thinking about it while talking to you. Somethings in life you just do things, but which you don't talk about Roger, I'm sure you understand that, you being a writer and all.

"But now that you know what the rooms are for, let me tell you how it works.

"If a woman wishes to avail herself of Home Deliveries, she makes a booking at the office when she first arrives and she is allocated a time slot, usually a two hour period to allow time for getting things sorted, along with the name of her room. By the way, she also nominates her preferred number of delivery boys; two, three or a maximum of four.

"The arrival of swipe plastic key cards has made life much easier. Her booking time and details are logged into the system and a message is sent to her mobile approving her so that she can use her card as an access key. Her access, by the way, is via doors in the Gals Only room."

Roger continued staring at Maria.

"So how are men selected to become the lucky delivery boys?"

"Well, again, the computer and magic swipe card takes care of everything.

"Men who have checked in to The Club that day, receive a message on their phones telling them that a female member has made a booking at Home Deliveries for a certain time and in a particular room. A man simply needs to send back a Yes if he is interested. A half hour before the start time, men are advised whether or not they have been allocated a delivery slot by the system's algorithm and if they have, the room name and the time.

"There is more. When more than one woman has booked in, and there could be a number during the day given that there are three booths and quite a few two-hour slots, details of all bookings are sent out to checked-in male members.

"Many men will reply Yes to all of them, improving their chances of getting selected for one. They cannot attend more than one each day. The computer analyses the data and sends out a confirmation to those selected a half-hour before the event is due to begin. There is an option for the men to cancel if they suddenly find themselves otherwise occupied. This enables the computer to issue another person with an invitation and issue the first man with another invitation if another Home Delivery event is available.

"It has all worked very well, so far.

"Does that help, Roger? Any questions?"

Roger was staring at Maria in wonder. Then Maria smiled and answered the look on Rogers face.

"Oh yes, of course there is. Maria laughed, self-consciously, "And the answer is yes, Roger. Twice in fact, and I must say that on both occasions, it was just what I needed. I'm sure more women would do it if only they knew how cathartic it can be.

"Some women I've spoken to think that they need it most at certain times of the month. This might be true."

With his brain in overload, Roger managed to look into Maria's eyes.

"I want to come to The Club with you Maria. Can we go on a Tuesday? I liked Tuesday's at The Club."

Maria took Roger's hand and leant forward and kissed him gently on the lips.

"Tuesday it is. And best of luck with Yvette. You will have to be really good to get that gorgeous creature to speak to you, let alone open her legs.

"And Roger! If all else fails and you can see that me and Veronica are not entertaining anyone, please feel free to come and bother us. I promise we'll do a good job of resisting your advances until we know we must surrender to you. That slut Veronica has already indicated that she wants your cock in her hand and her mouth and in other places too."

Maria started to leave, then stopped and said, "There are still a few things for you to learn about the club, Roger. I've just thought of a couple more.

"There is an unstated code of how the cinema is laid out and used by club members. I've already mentioned how the men hang around at the back and take up the first two rows of seats; rows one and two. Women never choose to sit in those rows.

"Rows ten, eleven and twelve at the front, you know about, and eight and nine are where women go who would prefer to be approached by women. This is not exclusively so, but it is what generally happens and it works very well. Veronica and I often sit in them when we are simply horny for some girl time.

"Rows four and five are known as Shy Way One and Two. They get their name from the fact that this is where the shy men sit. It is interesting how many men are nervous about approaching women and so this is where they sit. Some of them might be self conscious of their bodies, their weight for instance or think their penis is too small. And some might just prefer to be dominated.

"These rows are more popular with woman than one might think.

"The men sit in every other seat, where possible, leaving an empty seat on either side. A woman will cast her eye over the line-up and then go and sit beside the man of her choice and immediately open his fly if it isn't already open, and fondle him. She then either gets him off with her hand or mouth or sits on his cock and rides him. Neighbouring men will often join the couple, opening her bra and baring her breasts and groping her.

"For the woman in a hurry, it certainly beats waiting to be approached.

"Rows six and seven are multi purpose where anyone can approach anyone else. This is probably where the bulk of interactions take place.

"This brings me to the row some members call the Jungle, row three. You probably thought I'd missed it. Firstly, there is a walkway between row three and four, just as there is between rows nine and ten."

Roger took a deep breath, "My goodness, Maria. This is all fascinating information and it would take anthropologists years to document this level of detail while studying primitive peoples. But I'm interrupting, just as you sound as though you're getting to the good bit. Tell me about row three, Maria"

"I will paint you picture, Roger.

"I mentioned earlier that a number of a particular kind of women members looked down on the Home Deliveries booths. We might say that they are generally the wealthier and can I say, snobbier ones.

"We'll call them ladies, I'm sure they would like that. Anyway, imagine a couple of these ladies meeting for lunch and then wandering off to shop at designer shops and exclusive boutiques or visit their hairdresser. Later they pop home to their large houses with their shopping to hang it in her already extensively stocked walk-in wardrobe.

"The woman then removes her one-off designer clothes and showers and puts on a pleasant relatively inexpensive off-the-shelf outfit and drives back to her friends place. There they enjoy an hour or two of sitting beside the pool, nibbling hors d'oeuvres and drinking champagne.

"At around 3.30 they drive to the club in search of that little something they feel they need, to finish off the day. A bit of fun before dinner, telling each other that a girl needs a little fun, that something that they consider is missing in their life."

Roger found Maria's story wonderful, something he could never have written. It was a woman's point of view and he was loving it.

"The two happy ladies, thin and elegant in their light floral frocks and fancy frilly topped light coloured stockings and absurdly high-heeled sandals, enter the cinema hand in hand and then, after parading up and down the aisle like models on a cat-walk in a way that couldn't fail to get them noticed, they settle in seats two and three in row three. The Jungle row.

"One could probably hear the murmur of mens voices and feel the excitement in the air.

Maria looked at Roger and smiled, "Finding this yarn a bit of a turn-on Roger? I admit that I do."

"You bet I am Maria, so please don't stop."

Maria put her hand out and gently touched the lump in Roger's trousers and smiled her angelic smile.

"I think I better shorten the story, Roger.

"It is only moments before a hoard of males move in on the ladies. Very soon, their clothes have been removed and they are kneeling on their seats, minus their cheap skimpy underwear and with four men standing in the walkway taking turns with the rear ends of each of the women. The cock hungry ladies suck the juices from a half a dozen men facing them from behind their seats in row two who are happily groping the women's breasts while the ladies are swallowing their cum with great delight.

"Then two men will wriggle in under the women and the ladies will lower themselves onto stiff cocks while a man behind places his cock in the same stretched cunt or in between the cheeks of their elegant ladylike derrieres, looking for that other welcoming spot. Everything is performed in such a ladylike manner. Even their screams are ladylike, Roger."

Roger and Maria came together spontaneously, fucking like it was their first time.

"I'm happy to be your elegant lady bitch anytime, Roger. We don't need the Jungle. And I hope you will you have enough left to fuck my derriere, darling man? I would so enjoy that."

When the two stopped and laid back, happy and satisfied, Maria finished her story.

"So the ladies who decry the Home Deliveries as lower class

dogging, do in fact go dogging themselves, only in a slightly different way. But then, each to their own, I say."

Roger and Maria held each other close and caressed each other's bodies.

"I love making love with you Roger. Make love to me and Veronica together, soon please. I'm sure you will enjoy a threesome. I know we would."

Roger laughed and slapped Maria lovingly on her rear.

"How could a man refuse two such elegant ladies."

"I think I should go to the kitchen and make us a sandwich, Roger. You've made me hungry."

5

A SECOND VISIT

ROGER WAS EXCITED about his second visit to The Club. It wasn't just the thought of having an opportunity to communicate with Yvette. That was a challenge that he looked forward to. No! It was something else and he at last admitted to himself that he was at heart, a voyeur.

Watching people doing things that normally they would never do in public was sexually appealing and he accepted that there was an intellectual component although that would be hard to defend. A bit like saying you only looked at men's magazines for the articles.

On his first visit to The Club, Roger was slightly embarrassed to look closely at what was going on. It all seemed so personal and private. But now he realised that everyone in the movie theatre, both men and women, were there for pretty much the same reasons and that what one person was enjoying could be happily observed and even sometimes shared by anyone. Roger was ready for an adventure.

And of course there was the intellectual side of things. Watching something as rare as both sexes encouraging each other to display their base instincts was a very unusual event in our culture. In the past, only anthropologists had observed and written about these sort of behaviours in so called primitive peoples. Now Roger could see it at work in the comfort of a nearby mansion, just walking distance from his house.

Alvie at the front desk, welcomed Roger back.

"Well, young man. Rumour has it that you were a great success on your first visit; not naming names of course. Let's hope this week will be as successful."

Alvie pinned Roger's visitor number on his shirt, taking time to affectionately fiddle with his buttons and straighten his collar.

"Now if there is anything you need, just pop back out here to the kiosk, love. I'm here all day."

As Roger and Maria walked towards the cinema door, Veronica arrived. Roger hadn't really met her properly last week and it was in the dark, so it was a surprise to meet a very slim small youthful looking woman in a very tight fitting skirt and top along with the obligatory stockings with seams, and high heeled shoes. In different clothing she could easily have passed for a university student.

"Pleased to meet you properly, Roger. Maria will try to keep us apart. Selfish bitch! But feel free to sit beside me any time you need a break from your activities. Smaller bites of someone special like me can be just what you need when the bigger girls on offer become overwhelming.

"And you can simply be with me and rest if you want. Just so long as you hold my hand."

Roger enjoyed the woman's wit and, looking at the grinning Maria, replied enthusiastically that he looked forward to such an opportunity.

Roger found Veronica's face especially appealing. While everything about her was fine and petite, Veronica's large brown googly-eyes and her wide permanently open mouth displaying two rows of big bright white teeth and framed by her huge stretched-out cupid lips was a siren calling from the shore.

Roger could see that Yvette was not in the theatre, at least not yet, but looking around, he could see that things were starting to happen.

A couple of rows back, a man already had his hand inside a woman's wide open blouse and, without even glancing at him, she unbuttoned herself and lowered her bra to expose her nipples for him.

At the same time, she wriggled her backside as she lifted her skirt and reached up and pulled down her knickers. At least, that's what Roger thought he would be seeing if he was closer. Bad light and his rampant imagination could well be robbing him of the true situation, but he didn't mind one bit. He decided to take a closer look.

Roger nodded goodbye to his two lovely companions.

"Don't get into trouble Roger. Come back here for that."

Roger moved leisurely up the aisle, noticing other things happening in almost every row.

In one row close by, two women had uncovered their breasts and each was busily licking and sucking the other. Both were in the act of lifting their legs and pulling up their skirts to provide each other with even greater access to the more intimate parts of their hungry bodies; and their mutual heavy breathing and gasping was audible and, Roger thought, strangely reassuring.

Roger reached the row of seats where the activity that had first drawn his attention was in progress. The couple occupied seats two and three leaving one seat at each end of the row, empty. Roger sat down beside the woman, who, sensing his arrival looked across at him and smiled. Then Roger felt her hand on his trousers and he knew he was now part of the game.

Roger lifted himself up and pushed his trousers and underpants down around his knees, letting his penis stand up, seemingly searching around in the dim light to discover its whereabouts. A hand came and took his hand and placed it on a breast and rubbed the breast with it gently. Then the woman's head turned and looked down at Roger's lap and she immediately reached out and took hold of his penis and began to rub it up and down lovingly.

The man on the other side, let go and raised himself to also drop his trousers and pants to his knees, exposing himself as Roger had done and almost immediately, the lovely lady took hold of him. Then she turned to Roger and leant towards him and whispered, "Kiss me like you love me."

Roger put his spare hand behind the woman's head and pulled her gently to him and kissed her, at first most softly but then, as she responded, the two mouths opened to each other and their passion burst forth.

"Oh, my God. Kiss me like that again."

The woman grasped Roger's penis with a stronger grip. Then she let go of the other man and pulled up her skirt to display a neat little tuft of pubic hair. Then she rubbed herself and in a hushed sexy voice said, "Tell me how much you want to fuck me. You do want to fuck me don't you? You want to very much I know. Say it!"

Roger had no difficulty telling her that fucking her beautiful pussy was the thing he most wanted to do in life which he honestly felt to be true at that moment. At that point, the woman had shuddered, leaving his mouth just long enough to groan before fastening her mouth back on his.

"Come and do it to me now. Put your beautiful cock in my cunt. And don't stop kissing me, you beautiful bastard."

Roger suddenly noticed that another woman had arrived and seated herself at the other end and in just moments she had stolen the other fellows cock and was unbuttoning her shirt and dragging his hand to her breasts.

"All's fair in love and war." Roger thought as he moved down between his lovers stockinged legs. He deliberated about what he would do and what she expected him to do. If she was wanting a cock inside her then cunnilingus was probably not where he should go right now. He slid his cock into her moist vagina and the woman wriggled around.

"Bang me hard my darling. And don't stop kissing me till I cum."

Roger decided that given how she was already hot and excited, he would exercise his usual cock hard in and then hold his end tightly up against her pubic bone, not letting her move away from it. If she was already in a state of excitement similar to what results from cunnilingus, then all should work out to both their satisfaction. And it did.

With their mouths still locked in a never ending kiss, the woman came and then came again. And when she thought she should move back to let him thrust, he wouldn't let her move, and to her great surprise and great happiness, she came again and then again and just kept coming and in the end Roger heard her final exclamation of a great outcry of "Oh Yes!".

Their kissing ended and the woman slumped back in her seat. She gasped and then spoke.

"Oh yes! You really loved me, didn't you, you sexy bastard. Promise you will find me again. My name is Jasmine and I'm here on Tuesday's and Wednesdays. Thank you. That was truly beautiful."

Jasmine rested her hand on Roger face and happily held his still monumental cock.

"You are beautiful Jasmine," replied Roger, purposely forgetting to offer his name. But then he noticed her looking at his visitor number.

"I will remember you number twenty-eight, and I will make sure that you and I go to heaven again. Thank you."

6

GETTING THE HANG OF THINGS

ROGER HAD NOT REALLY LOOKED at the male members of The Club. This might have been because, as a boy one didn't look at the other boys when they were in the changing room after sports. To do so would have attracted unkind comments and elicit aspersions about ones masculinity. And given that most of the men here at The Club had their cocks in their hands as they fiddled around working out what to do next, to look too closely at them could have been embarrassing for both parties.

Two things set the men apart from the average collection of blokes. The first thing was that they were all well dressed and seemingly well off. The second thing was that they were all older men. Even though the joining age for men had been lowered to forty-five, men below sixty were not much in evidence. Roger noted that these older men looked very fit. Most looked as though they exercised regularly and most appeared sun tanned.

Roger guessed that the lack of younger men could be because they were at work during the week, not yet having retired from their jobs. Given that The Club was open every day except Sunday, he wondered if Saturday was when younger men showed up.

There seemed to always be a few men standing up at the back or spread out on the back two rows of seats who seemed happy to just be rubbing their cocks while watching the movie and Roger wondered if, and at what point any of them chose to interact with the horny ladies in the rows further down.

Roger sauntered back down to where Maria and Veronica where sitting, realising as he approached that the two women were not alone. What appeared to be the same two women that Roger had observed making love further up the aisle earlier, had now moved to be on their knees in front of Maria and Veronica. His friends lay back with their eyes closed and their lovely breasts on display. They held their beautiful legs up and wide apart and bent at the knees. Two heads were moving rhythmically between their legs, totally absorbed and slurping with great enthusiasm.

Veronica sensed Roger's presence and opened her eyes and looked up at him and smiled lazily.

"Show me your cock, Roger. I was just dreaming about you. Let me suck you."

Roger undid his belt and let his trousers drop to the floor and then he pushed down his underpants to join them. His cock was still rampant and Veronica's mouth dropped open.

"Oh Roger. You've been a naughty boy haven't you. Where has this been, I wonder. I can smell something nice. What a lucky lady; but she didn't finish you off, Roger?"

Veronica reached out and took Roger's cock in her hand.

"You distinctly told me, Veronica. Don't get into trouble. Come back here for that."

The two laughed, enjoying the gentle joke.

"Oh Roger, you are such a darling. May I finish you off now? I think I should before you get into any more trouble."

Maria opened her eyes and looked across at the two beside her, saw what they were doing and smiled.

"Oh you lucky slut, Veronica, he came back just for you. I'm very jealous."

Roger felt the small hand of Veronica and moments later, she opened her bright red lips and her mouth took charge. Her mouth movements were divine and it wasn't long before Roger erupted deep in her throat.

Veronica's big eyes smiled loving up at him as she gulped and then she held and lovingly licked his cock. As she did so, her flashing eyes moved back under her eyelids and her body stiffened and she gasped as the woman between her legs reached that certain point of no return. Veronica came and Maria came moments later, and the two ladies who had given them both such happiness, clasped each other and fell back on the floor, rubbing each other and calling out.

Veronica came out of her orgasmic trance and looked up at Roger.

"Promise me we'll do that again, Roger. I could happily suck your cock for ever. You are definitely the man I've been looking for."

7

MEETING THE CLUB OWNER

DESLEY HAD ARRIVED home from her overseas business trip. She contacted Maria and asked her to arrange for Roger to come and see her. She said that Saturday morning at around eleven would be a good time.

Roger thought about The Club membership. With huge numbers of women and men working, it was likely that many now worked five days a week right into their later years, but Roger wasn't drawing any conclusions about the age spread just yet. It also occurred to him that quite a number of the wealthy sun tanned older men he'd seen on his earlier visits might be spending time on yachts in Sydney harbour, either their own or a friends.

Roger was a half hour early and the friendly smile from Alvie in the office was welcoming.

"Busy day, Saturdays. I hope you can find something to your liking."

Alvie giggled as she pinned his number onto his shirt. She stared at Roger and Roger wondered what this woman did when she wasn't working. Did she have a husband, perhaps?

Roger wandered into the cinema. Most of the seats were taken and it was soon apparent that some of those who could only comfortably get to The Club on a Saturday, were making up for their lack of access during the week.

Womens heads were bobbing up and down or backwards and forwards while other's had their legs waving in the air while their breasts were being groped and their mouth were sucking on cocks offered to them from the rows behind, their free hands rubbed the cocks of those sitting either side of them. One knelt on her seat as a man shafted her from the back while she rubbed and sucked the two men standing at the back of the seat.

There was a buzz of activity and Roger thought how much it reminded him of when the honey-flow happened in the huge gum tree at his front gate.

There was much more action today compared to what Roger had witnessed on his previous week-day visits. He thought how much more active the women were and noted that they all seemed to be happily engaged, much more noticeably than what he had observed on week days. He pondered if this might be an example of presence of younger members or was it herd mentality, where once a certain number were doing something, then everyone runs off in the same direction, or in this case, everyone rushes to open their bras and their legs.

Roger scanned the cinema for Yvette and it was only at the last moment he spied her and his heart gave a little thump. But then he realised that, firstly, he was on his way to a meeting, and secondly Yvette was sitting in the second row from the front meaning she had placed herself off limits. But then he was happy about where she was sitting.

Roger then wandered up to the entrance door but he still had about fifteen minutes before his interview with Desley, so he turned right and headed towards the room signposted as The Parlour. The room was beautifully furnished and provided six cubicles, each with a large sofa bed along with small fine touches such as a vase of fresh flowers and jugs of fresh water with fresh cut lemons floating in it. There was a black and white framed print on each cubicle wall. Roger noted that each print was from a collection he had seen in a large volume of work entitled 'Erotic Art From the 17th to the twentieth century', and collected for an exhibition in Frankfurt in 1995.

Each room had its own door and blinds making it totally private. Roger heard loving sounds coming from one cubicle that had its door shut and he thought that this would be the place where he would like to bring Yvette should the opportunity ever arise.

Meeting Desley was a great pleasure. The very fine looking older woman smiled at Roger and began by congratulating him on "a certain successful interaction with one of our most respected members".

Roger murmured something about it being his pleasure and he was glad the client had enjoyed it too.

As the two talked, Desley sat behind her large wooden desk holding a pen and occasionally writing on a pad. Maria had told Roger that Desley was in her mid sixties but she could very easily pass for someone at least ten years younger.

"Now, Roger, I've read your book and I've heard a little about your recent exploits and so far, I'd say that you seem to tick all the boxes that will lead to me offering you the job of writing up the story of The Club. I assume we should start with you asking me questions. Is that what you would want, Roger?"

"Yes, Desley, we can start there. We should start by being brief, at least me in my questioning. We can expand on things later. And the first question must be what led you to want to start a female-friendly adult cinema club?"

"Well, Maria might have told you that I run a charity for older and unemployed, pre pension age sex workers. Raising money is not that easy. It's not a cause you can easily sell raffle tickets for or advertise. There isn't a strong sympathetic public to exploit.

"I was looking for something new, then I remembered visiting a porn cinema in London many years ago and being shocked at how awful it was even though at the same time, I was intrigued. It was just a place for desperado's and lonely pervs and the few women that I saw visiting were indeed a sad lot.

"I forgot about it for a long time, then one day I was talking to my brother Arnold who reminded me that he had the finest collection of blue movies on the planet, completely catalogued and cross-reference every which way, and how it was a pity we couldn't capitalise on them.

"It was then that the idea was born. And it fitted in nicely with the philosophy that I was developing regarding womens empowerment. As you know I've always been close to what is generally known as the sex industry but which I prefer to label "essential personal needs services".

Roger watched the relaxed woman, enjoying her facial expressions and easy movements.

"So, Desley, if I might interrupt. In trying to understand the essence of things, what I most want to know is what motivates women to join The Club. In other words, what is on offer that they haven't had access to previously.

And I have a second part of the same question, namely, if - and I emphasise the word if - the excitement for a woman derives from anticipation of something pleasurable but unexpected happening, this means that such events cannot be prearranged because they only work if they are spontaneous.

Roger paused and looked at Desley.

"Well done Roger. You are right on the mark with your question and the answers are not simple but have their roots in an amalgam of elements.

"Firstly, lets talk about the movies. A woman visits The Club knowing that she can sit for as long as she like in complete comfort watching erotic movies. In itself, this is exciting for a woman. She can watch other women be a part of a narrative that, while it is usually predictable, still offers a female viewer the excitement of illicit and taboo action in a darkened room where, if she is so inclined, she can entertain herself with her hands and fingers. I should add that a number of female members never want anything more than to come to watch the movies, ignoring or rebutting moves by males and females to involve them in anything else.

"This is why I instigated the women and couples only front three rows.

"So that is number one.

"Secondly, a woman wants to be wanted and also adored. If being wanted coincides with her already feeling horny from watching a movie, and then being surprised by a would-be suitor touching her arm, then she is given an opportunity to play a game. We could say it's a version of flirting. Resisting the persistent male until he either leaves or triggers a positive response whereby she accepts, in part, some of his or in some cases, her advances. Punishing or encouraging her suitor to make him even more interested is historically part of a woman's game play. It provides proof of the man's serious intent."

Roger moved forward on his chair.

"Let me interrupt you there for a moment. I hear what you say but I can't help feeling that at The Club, there must eventually be an "Oh, not you again," moment as the women confront their suiters.

"I'd like you to address that, Desley."

"Your point was definitely something I worried about a lot when we started and fortunately, the growth of membership has helped considerably. But your question is still valid and I can only give you the answer I came up with.

"Remembering that my interest is in making a place for women to enjoy helps to understand that I am not too fussed about how men react. Not that I don't want the men to enjoy themselves. It's simply that men have a different take on things entirely because of the way their bodies work. They will do whatever it takes to satisfy themselves and not necessarily at The Club. Their drive is simply to touch a female's private parts or be touched by her.

"Coming back to your question, you might not know this but there are twice as many male members of The Club than females. However, the men are restricted to alternate days access which switches each week. For example, if you were rostered for Monday, Wednesday and Friday this week, you are rostered on for Tuesday, Thursday and Saturday the following week.

"This not only provides a much greater number of males for the women to choose from, rotating them means they also know that a man they saw at The Club last Wednesday won't be back there at least until Wednesday fortnight. Women can to a certain degree avoid a person or seek him out. Whatever their intent. So far this has worked well but I'm for ever watching how we can improve things."

This was new to Roger and he was impressed.

"Wow! No, I didn't know that and it certainly sounds like a practical solution to a number of possible hiccups that I can now stop worrying about.

"So now, let me ask about the age of club members. I understand it is currently fifty for women and forty-five for men. So should I presume that the lower age for men is to offset the likely reduced physicality of the older males? Or have I got it wrong? By the way, I have already ascertained that many of the men are taking one of the erection enhancement drugs prior to their visit to the club.

Desley looked kindly at Roger and smiled her wonderful older women-come-motherly smile that so easily excited Roger.

"Yes. Libido is something that we have only limited control of. In fact we have no control other than providing the various enhancements at the kiosk along with a range of dildos in the Gals Room and Parlour.

"Just as an aside, in the early days, we considered putting in a Glory Hole facility. You can probably quickly foresee the problems. A plentiful supply of volunteering strong large cocks would be needed which would require younger men, and given The Club's membership age range, this just wasn't going to happen.

"In some ways, the Home Deliveries room has provided a sort if alternative to the Glory Hole. It's appeal fits a similar group of enthusiasts. The room is slowly becoming more popular but the stigma of what goes on there is probably going to last for some time. On the bright side, it means that we are catering for a wider audience which must, in the end, be a good thing."

Roger chuckled and Desley looked at him quizzically, and asked what was amusing.

"Well I've heard that some woman now refer to it as The Bitchery, partly due to the idea of bitches coming on season.

"It was also mentioned that observations suggested that some women following a monthly cycle in their usage which fitted the in-season concept. Not sure why I'm telling you this but I thought it was interesting.

Desley laughed heartily.

"Well, that's new to me and I do appreciate you telling me. It's amazing what you can miss if you are away for a while.

"I've just being going through the letters in the suggestion box. I sometimes think it was a mistake putting it there at the front counter, but never mind.

"It seems from the letters, that a number of female members would like a service that offered them a cock in a private location so that they could satisfy their cock sucking desires. There are some of them, apparently, who would like to meet up with a man who was happy to volunteer to be sucked for at least a good half hour or more. Some men, it seems are in too much of a hurry. They say that getting a good suck is difficult in the theatre and ideally there would be a service that the computer could administer, similar to Home Deliveries.

"As it happens, we do have an unused spare room so I'll think about it.

"Now, next question, Roger?"

"Right! Now I've read the Guidelines for Membership and found them both comprehensive and impressive. All of the points are made clearly and I have no questions arising from them.

"So for the moment, you have satisfied both my curiosity and my need for information. My suggestion is that I take the outline of what you want me to write and come back to you with a point-by-point outline of what I believe I should write.

"While writing the article looks straight forward, I think we might have to talk through some of the sociological or psychological questions - particularly about women - that we've touched on, just to be sure we both understand what we are wanting to convey.

"There are a couple of deep philosophical questions regarding human behaviour that are worth discussing even though no conclusions can be made, nor could references to the studies be mentioned. I refer to recent works on the social lives of the Bonobo monkeys who live under a matriarchal system, and how one can draw parallels with human female behaviour and the Bonobos.

"If you are interested, I could drop some reading matter in to you. I would love to hear your thoughts on the subject.

"So! Why don't I come back to you with something this time next week, Desley. And after you've looked at it, you can decide if you think I'm the person for the job."

The beautiful Desley smiled broadly at Roger and stood up and came around to his side of the desk.

"I think I've already decided that you are the one, Roger. But yes, come back next week and we can discuss things, including your payment."

Desley came close to Roger and put a hand on his arm and stared into his eyes.

"The Mayoress said you were a wonderful kisser, Roger. Because of my work and position I have very little opportunity for any sort of social life on the side, so to speak, and I do miss some things. I would appreciate it if you kissed me Roger. And I promise that if you can't do that, it will not affect our business relationship."

Roger was unprepared for this moment and he wasn't really sure how much kissing Desley's words implied. But he responded as was befitting a younger man being invited to attend a special party.

Roger put his arms gently around the well built Desley and drew her to him, all the time looking into her smiling eyes. Roger put his hand behind the woman's head placed his lips on hers and in moments Desley opened up her mouth and the two tongued each other.

Then Desley took Rodger's hands and slid them down over her tight skirt and her very large buttocks. Then she pulled his head down and thrust it into the cleavage Roger had tried desperately not to stare at during their meeting. Roger could smell apples and peaches, and Disney's breasts felt just like ripe peaches as he ventured to touch them with his tongue.

Roger could feel the woman's solid buttocks through her dress and moments later he felt her hands rubbing the very large lump in his trousers. The two clung on to each other and groped one another for some time. Desley sometimes pulled back her head and gasped then quickly sought out Roger's mouth for more kissing.

Roger was about to start unbuttoning Desley skirt but the woman called a halt to their adventure, putting her finger to his lips and nodding her head from side to side.

"We will have a relaxed time together later, you beautiful man. My voluptuous body is wanting to be your stairway to heaven Roger, and I promise it will. Don't forget me."

8

SOMETIMES A DISAPPOINTMENT

DESLEY HAD GIVEN Roger full visiting rights for The Club. She smilingly suggested that she wouldn't like to think he was missing out on any of life's essential nourishments. While doing his research he would have every opportunity for erotic dalliances and she said that she expected him to sample them all. Only for his research of course.

It was only to be expected that Roger's erotic disposition would be heightened when he wandered around The Club. He was still trying to answer the question definitively what excited women and drew them to use The Club. In particular what attracted them to accept the advances of men they'd never met before. Men's motivation was an open book. They were driven by mother natures simple programming that ensured that eggs got fertilised, regardless. Women on the other hand, were expected to treat the fertilisation of their eggs with greater thought and responsibility. But then perhaps modernity had changed women's perception of their sexual role? And of course, older women need not play by those rules. More questions than answers seemed to be the proper take on this topic.

Roger reasoned that he needed to put himself into the situation where a woman - any woman - would either reject or accept him. He needed to go in cold and attempt to seduce someone. He smiled to himself as he heard himself say "for research purposes, of course".

It was mid-afternoon and the cinema was quite busy. Men populated the back rows, some holding their exposed cocks and watching the movie whilst also keeping an eye on the activities of the women in the rows in front.

Roger stood at the back and surveyed the scene. A voice inside him barked instructions. It told him to just get on with it and walk down and approach the first woman who was alone. In the end, Roger did just that.

Sitting beside a woman wearing a buttoned-up rain coat wasn't difficult. But what next? As Roger lowered himself into the seat beside her, the woman glanced across at him but gave no acknowledgement, no hint of a smile or even a nod. Then she turned back to continue staring at the cinema screen.

Roger put the woman's age at between fifty-five and sixty. She was thin and her face had that hint of someone who regularly enjoyed a drink or maybe two or three in the evening before bed. Roger believed that whatever people might say, women who drink regularly are more likely to show a deterioration of their body and particularly their facial features than do men; and there was also a cigarette smoke odour, which to his mind wasn't conducive to love-making.

Roger settled into his seat, noticing the thin shiny stockinged legs and the high heeled shoes, showing below the woman's coat. He could smell a perfume mixed in with the cigarette smell which was not unpleasant. Roger ventured a quick glance and he saw that her small mouth was tight and her lips were thin.

Roger waited, wondering what length of time would be appropriate before he made a first move. After what he thought was an acceptable passage of time, Roger put his hand across and touched and gently rubbed the woman's upper arm. He expected an initial rebuff but that didn't happen. Instead, a few moments later, the woman slowly reached up and begun to unbutton her rain coat, her bejewelled fingers flashing as her rings caught the light from the cinema screen. When she stopped, Roger looked and saw that she had exposed a black bra covering a pair of small breasts. Then the woman turned her head and with a stony look at Roger, seemed to indicate that she had made him an offer he couldn't refuse.

Roger hesitated but then he responded. He leant over and began unbuttoning the rest of the woman's coat as she continued to stare ahead of her. Then Roger pulled back the raincoat to expose her fully, not expecting to discover that the women was wearing neither a skirt nor panties, seeing just a suspender belt and her stockings.

Wondering what the woman would like him to do next or what she expected him to do, occupied Roger's mind for just a moment. Then he reminded himself that to make this totally real, he should be asking himself what he wanted and not be too concerned about her choices. She would express herself in whatever way she felt inclined too.

He placed a hand on a bra cup and rubbed gently, feeling a nipple beneath the satin. Then, with a bent index finger, Roger pulled the bra down on both sides and exposed two upright nipples on tiny flat breasts and instinctively he leant over and took each in turn into his mouth and sucked and nibbled them.

His attention to her nipples seemed not to register with the woman. She remained stony faced and staring at the screen. Roger wondered if he should kiss her but wasn't drawn to the idea for some reason. Her unresponsive manner and his own lack of desperation seemed to add up to a complete non event. Not that Roger thought that his activities so far had been especially romantic or erotically motivating.

Various scenarios crossed Roger's mind as he pondered the situation. Was he already sexually too well nourished? Was he being too stereotypical in his approach? Was the chemistry between them simply wrong? Was he just not showing signs of needing her attention? Suddenly, all was revealed.

Another male arrived and sat on the other side of the woman. His fly was open and his cock was upright and waving about. He placed his lips on hers and his hand plunged in between her legs. The woman reached for the man's cock and rubbed it vigorously and just moments later she pulled him over in between her legs and fed him into her vagina. Then she began to heave her backside up and forward to meet his frantic thrusting and in a few moment, the man erupted and moments later he had disappeared.

All that Roger had witnessed had happened very quickly. Just as he was reviewing his situation, another man arrived with his cock waving in the air. And again, the woman took hold of it and rubbed it vigorously then pulled it down in between her legs and the same scenario was repeated. As the man was about to leave, he announced in a low voice that he would "See you in the Primrose room shortly, Lola."

As Roger moved slowly up the aisle, the woman he had just been with, pushed past him and he watched as she disappeared headed towards the Gals Only room. Roger knew that Lola was heading off to meet her delivery boys and he couldn't help wondering how many there would be.

A voice from not far away called out "Go Lola," and the tone suggested that the caller knew the woman intimately.

Roger decided that this was not his finest hour. He was out of his league and that it would be wise to move away, shouldering the brutal image of his failure.

In many ways, Roger felt relieved. Maybe he hadn't failed after all. Rather he just hadn't succeeded where in fact he should never have been in the first place. He was never going to be enough for Lola. She obviously knew what erotic experiences she wanted and it definitely included nothing like what Roger was fumbling around with. Roger had to admit, he just wasn't hardcore enough.

9

REMEMBERING THE LADIES OF POSITANO

ROGERS LIFE HAD DEFINITELY BECOME MORE hectic since accepting the job of writing up The Club prospectus.

Life at home had become second to the new writing task and even the moments with Caroline on Skype seemed remote to his senses. Caroline said that her belly was now a noticeable bump but that she was feeling super healthy. She was due back in Australia in about a month and laughingly suggested that she would be well and truly ready for his cock, or – daddy-thing – as she was now calling it, when she arrived home.

Roger hoped to have The Club project totally off his plate by then. Desley was happy with the finished manuscript suggesting only a few minor adjustments which he had done. The typesetting had been completed except for the corrections and the interesting collection of photos had been strategically placed through the text.

Arnold had been put in charge of processing and enhancing the pictures a few of which were taken surreptitiously by Desley inside a porn bookshop cinema in Brixton. It showed the abject horror of that level of adult entertainment, contrasting it with coloured photographs of the beautiful interior of The Club.

As a document that Desley wanted to use to sell the concept to franchisee's around the globe, it contained enough to wet appetites but not the full details of the management structure. Those details would be available to people who bought a franchise along with her and Arnold's personal attention where needed.

Caroline had asked Roger on Skype, how he was going with the project. He had mentioned it to her after they had had a conversation about money when he wanted to let her know that he did get other work apart from the books he'd had published. However, he'd thought twice about telling her everything about The Club, only that it was an expensive private club. Roger was pleased that she hadn't bothered to ask for more details.

The day came when Desley called Roger to say that she had a cheque for him and that she wanted to give it to him in person at The Club on the upcoming Sunday afternoon. They would have the place entirely to themselves, she said.

"I've long wanted to play out the part of a club member, she said over the phone in her seductive mellow voice. I hope you will indulge me, Roger. In fact, it would be the perfect time to play out a fantasy from your second novel that got me so excited."

Roger thought for a moment. He guessed what Desley was referring to. That was the bit he had had a bit of bother with his editor over the subject of incest but by making the protagonists very distant relatives helped get it through.

Suddenly, the idea appealed to Roger although he wasn't certain why. Was it for the right or wrong reasons, he wondered. Followed by, but what were the right reasons?

"Let me guess which part, Desley. You would like me to play uncle Luigi and you be Carlotta?"

"Yes!" came back Desley's emphatic reply. Would you do that for your little university student five-times removed niece? She so wants it."

"We don't have her two wicked aunts to hold her down on that first occasion that her uncle does naughty things to her, unfortunately."

"Just talk me through it when the time comes you dunderhead, laughed the now excited voice at the other end of the phone. And by the way, will Luigi be happy to cope with a much larger uni student I wonder?"

"I'm sure he will welcome a size increase, dear lady. I just happen to know that he would."

Desley giggled excitedly down the phone.

"Can we say three o'clock on Sunday afternoon. I'll leave the main door open and you can lock it from the inside. I'll be in the cinema down in row four. See you then, uncle Luigi."

When Roger walked into The Club on Sunday afternoon, he noted how eerily quiet it was. The hushed tension and hint of excitement that permeated the place when you came in on other days was missing. But that didn't matter. Roger knew where to find what he was looking for.

What no one but Roger knew about the Luigi and Carlotta incident - even his editor - was that it was based on an event that really happened to him when he was in Italy.

Loving exploits with older Italian ladies in black and organised by his delightful older woman friend and lover Martina, in Positano, had included monthly visits to the Rossi sisters, Giulia and Arianna. Giulia and Arianna were in their mid fifties and were of independent means, owning quite a number of cottages and two trattoria and a ristorante in the region. Neither had felt any need to marry. Their strong female bodies enjoyed whoever they selected to bring home, be they a man or a woman.

The Rossi sisters made quite a fuss of Martina's friend Roger when he came to visit and he occasionally wondered whether he had the stamina to keep going, swapping between the two pairs of legs waving at him from on high, one pair skinny and the other pair plump, both in shiny black stockings and beating the air in anticipation while the two excitedly called out who-knows-what in Italian. But Roger had quite early in life, learnt to forego his own orgasms in favour of a yogic withholding strategy, giving him the opportunity of being able to enjoy lovemaking for an extended period and this ability served him well when he visited the sisters.

One day when Roger arrived at the Rossi house for a weekend visit, he was pleasantly surprised to find that a young woman was staying with them. The constantly smiling girl was a student at the University of Salerno at Fisciano and she was the daughter of a distant relative of the Rossi family. She was a big well-built girl who hadn't learnt about the pitfalls of eating too much pasta, nor the difficulties of fitting into her blue and white check student skirt and long white socks; and her bulging blouse verged on the indecent, or at least that is how Roger saw it, or perhaps one should say, appreciated it.

Roger was introduced to the young woman by the sisters in very broken english but fortunately, the young Carlotta spoke perfect english and immediately took over proceedings. Carlotta listened to her aunts enthusiastic commentary then looked at Roger.

"My aunts speak very highly of you, sir," Then the young woman coloured up and grinned as she decoded the aunts' ongoing discussion.

"What are they saying, Carlotta?"

The red faced young woman lowered her eyes to the floor then murmured that she preferred not to say because she thought it was too personal.

That evening at dinner, the Sangiovese flowed and the housekeeper served a sumptuous meal and all were merry and bright.

The women had dressed up in their finery and Giulia and Arianna seemed intent on impressing on their young visitor the forbidden carnal delights that a grown-up woman deserved to enjoy. At least that is what Roger seemed to pick up from the raucous laughter and banter and the fact that Carlotta's face was bright red most of the time and that the large girl - bulging in her tight clothing - seemed never sure whether to laugh or cry.

It was later in the evening, when the dishes had been cleared away, and when Arianna came around to Roger and made him move his chair out from the table before putting her hand on his trousers, that things began to hot up. Giulia followed, dragging a protesting Carlotta with her.

Roger admitted to himself that he had drunk more than he had planned. He seemed to find himself grinning stupidly at all three ladies and moments later he looked down to see Arianna holding his cock and waving it at the confused Carlotta who had been pushed down to kneel with her head close to Rogers proudly waving member.

The wild-eyed Carlotta and her aunt Giulia watched as Arianna put Roger into her mouth and sucked him. Then the two pulled Carlotta's head over him and Arianna pulled Roger's cock up to touch Carlotta's lips while Giulia held the girls head firmly in position to complete the task at hand. Roger felt Carlotta's lips open and her mouth slowly take him in and then the two tipsy sisters cheered and congratulated Carlotta on her first cock sucking adventure.

The Rossi sisters moved away to find and refresh their glasses and Roger stared down at the source of the beautiful feeling on his cock. Then he felt the young woman's mouth let go and she lifted her head and looked up at him with her pretty face smiling coyly and whispered, "Am I doing it right, Roger?"

Roger assured Carlotta that what she was doing was indeed being done right. "You are sucking me beautifully, Carlotta. I love it," he whispered back. Carlotta smile broadened and she went back to her sucking, even venturing to run an exploratory hand under his testicles and lovingly rub his balls.

It was only a short time before the sisters returned. They stood and smiled at the now enthusiastic girl's head moving rhythmically up and down. Then they looked at Roger and one said, "Is good? Si?" Then they whispered in Carlotta's ear and the girl stopped sucking and stood up and smiled lovingly down at Roger.

"I think we are expected on their bed, Roger. I will if you will?"

As the sisters marched Carlotta down the passage way to the bedroom, Roger lifted himself up onto his feet and followed. He attempted to think about what was happening but didn't get very far.

Giulia appeared and took his hand and led him to the bedroom. Arianna lay on the bed holding Carlotta's head between her legs. The young woman seemed to be enjoying herself and Giulia left Roger and joined them. First she removed the kneeling Carlotta's blue and white check skirt and her knickers, displaying the girls very large and beautiful rear end including her near-hairless and deliciously plump pussy.

Then she pushed her face into the girls very slippery looking vagina and ravished her with her mouth.

Roger stood at the side of the bed desperately trying to focus. The only part of him that seemed to function was his stiff penis which, unusually, seemed impervious to the effects of the alcohol. He thought he felt hands guiding him onto the bed but that was definitely the last thing he recalled.

When Roger woke in the early hours, he found himself in the bed and cuddled up to the gorgeous soft body of the naked Carlotta. The young woman was sleeping soundly while holding Roger's half erect cock with one hand while the other propped up a large breast near Rogers lips.

A gentle exploration with his hand discovered that one of the sisters had a hand between Carlotta's wide open thighs and the other hand held one of her sisters breasts. All were happily sleeping.

Roger had obviously passed out and missed the party.

Roger yawned and lamented his absence from whatever happened. Then he smiled and reasoned that if the women had enjoyed their time with him when he wasn't really there, then it was likely that they would all be happy to do it again, even if only to show him what he had missed.

And things turned out exactly as he had thought and that evening the performance had been repeated only with Roger definitely less inebriated and fully awake.

Before Carlotta left a couple of days later, and when the sisters had taken a trip to the shops, the young woman came up close and said to Roger that, while they were alone and because she was leaving that afternoon, would he please take her back into the bedroom and make love to her. She said she wanted it without the assistance or interference of the sisters to which he replied in the affirmative as he took the earnest young woman's hand and led her to the bed.

First Roger enjoyed exploring Carlotta's delightful body. There wasn't a spot where he would have been happy just rubbing himself against her. And he delighted in licking those chubby and prominent parts surrounding her pussy. But he knew the two had only a limited window of opportunity and he led the charge with his cunnilingus act, watching the flesh on her delightful big body shake and move around. He followed with his hard-in penis finale. Carlotta screamed and threw herself about and clung tightly to Roger as she experienced a series of multiple orgasms.

When they had finished and were lying back on the sisters' big bed, Carlotta announced that she was going to come down and visit regularly. But then she was silent for a moment. Then she asked Roger where he lived. And when he gave his address at Positano, she excitedly turned to him and asked if she could come and fuck him at the weekends, to which he replied that much as he loved the idea, he was only there for another three weeks as he was returning to London.

Carlotta was at first devastated but then she laughingly commented that maybe her aunts would find her another nice cock like his. Then, as she pondered all the options, Carlotta announced, "And in the meantime, you can do me a lot of times in three weeks, Roger."

Roger grudgingly confessed that her getting introduced to another nice cock by her aunts was all very likely, and that three weekends of fucking the large young woman would suit him just fine.

10

GETTING BEHIND WITH HIS WORK

WHEN ROGER WALKED down the aisle to be with Desley, he couldn't have imagined how things would be.

Laying back in her seat, Desley was a picture of Roger's erstwhile dreams of Carlotta.

Desley had pulled up her blue and white check skirt displaying her large white legs and her cotton tails, the crotch of which her hand was gently massaging. Her white blouse was unbuttoned and pulled right back displaying her giant breasts standing like vanilla blancmanges and displaying a pair of nipples that were set in a large circle of pinky-brown flesh that called out for Roger's mouth.

Desley looked up at Roger lovingly.

"I've even shaved my pussy, uncle Luigi."

Roger looked down on the scene and, as had happened to him in the recent past, he slipped happily into another epiphanous moment and believed he was really with the now carnally enlightened Carlotta.

"Well, Carlotta. What will uncle Luigi do first to his beautiful girl? Maybe he should kiss her."

Roger's time in Italy had provided him with a believable Italian accent

Roger bent over Desley and found her willing mouth and they

tongued each other, passionately, just as Carlotta had kissed him after she had discovered how much she had enjoyed his cock for the first time. As he did so, each hand moved on to Carlotta's huge breasts and took hold of a nipple and tugged them upwards. Then he took turns sucking on them.

"Oh, uncle, I'm feeling strange all over. Will you show me your cock, please uncle?"

Roger unzipped his trousers and removed them. Then he took hold of Desley's hand and wrapped her fingers around his member, feeling her tremble and gasp with excitement.

"Now uncle Luigi wants Carlotta's beautiful pussy."

Roger knelt down between Desley's legs and did his cunnilingus thing. Unconsciously, he wasn't expecting a big reaction, considering Desley's age and likely vast experience, but her large body began to heave and tremble and suddenly she pushed herself up against his face and came, yelling, "Oh yes, uncle. Yes!".

"What a darling girl you are, Carlotta. Uncle wants to fuck your pussy now, you beautiful little slut."

Roger removed his cock from Desley's hand and slipped it inside her welcoming cunt. He looked at her beautiful countenance and thought how peaceful she appeared, her eyes were closed and her mouth was slightly open, breathing in and out as he slowly shagged her.

"Give me a nipple you naughty girl. I want to bite you."

Immediately, Desley thrust a giant nipple at his mouth and Roger gorged on it. Roger slowed and then did his hard fuck trick, holding his member hard up against the top of Desley's large hairless mons and not letting her back off. Desley squirmed and tried to get away, but then she let out a scream.

"Oh, uncle Luigi. You are fucking me to heaven. Don't stop."

Desley pulled her breast from Roger's mouth and pulled his head to hers and smothered him with wet kisses.

"Oh, God! This is so beautiful uncle. Tell me you will want to fuck your little slut again like this. Say it, Uncle Luigi."

Roger waited a few moments. Then speaking as uncle Luigi, he answered.

"If, when I roll you over and fuck your beautiful arse Carlotta, and you tell me that you love it, then I will decide if we should do this again."

Desley shook with excitement, "Oh my goodness, I soo love this."

Roger waited a little longer, letting Desley come again from his hard-in shagging. Then he made his next move.

"Now you horny little bitch, let uncle roll you over and sample your other wares. His cock is hungry for what you are hiding from him between your beautiful buttocks. Tell him you want it. Go on, say it."

Desley was squirming, torn between wanting a final orgasm before Roger withdrew, and the excitement that uncle Luigi was suggesting he wanted to do to her bottom.

Carlotta squeaked her reply.

"Oh, yes please uncle. I've been dreaming of you fucking my big lonely bottom. Do it to me, uncle Luigi."

Roger looked down on the totally enraptured woman and he leant forward and kissed her passionately. Desley groaned and thrust her tongue into his mouth. But then he let her go and rolled her gently over onto her tummy and then he lifted her so that her knees where on the floor and her backside looked up at the ceiling.

Roger looked down on a backside like no other he'd seen since Carlotta's.

Even at her age, Desley had managed to keep her body in very good shape and her rear-end was flawless. He was about to reach for the tiny bottle of lubricant, but then, when he parted Desley's buttocks he saw that the shiny pink anus had already had a visit from a lubricating squeegee.

Roger rubbed his cock up and down the crack between Disney's buttock cheeks while at the same time, reaching right round the large woman's hips to cup her chubby pussy in his hand. He fondled it gently and gently bit into Disney's neck. The woman shuddered and moaned and muttered something but he couldn't make out what. Then she called out.

"Oh uncle Luigi! I love you so much. Please put your tongue in where you want to put your cock and make me a very happy girl. Oh yes, uncle, give me more please."

Roger obliged, licking Desley beautiful anus and dribbling saliva into it.

"Now, Carlotta. Uncle's Luigi is having your backside. Are you ready?"

"Oh yes, uncle. Do it to me, please."

Roger's cock slipped easily into the cavernous backside doorway. It briefly crossed his mind that he was traveling down a well-worn tunnel and that Desley had enjoyed anal sex for a very long time.

Roger had been happily having his way in Disney's secret place, almost forgetting he was uncle Luigi. Then came Carlotta's voice.

"Uncle Luigi?"

Roger took his time inside Desley beautiful arse. It was a truly wonderful place to be and he really would have liked to stay there for longer.

"Yes, Carlotta. What is it?"

"I want to get you off uncle. Please let me."

There was a silence as Roger considered the offer. He would be happy to come here in her beautiful backside but he knew he shouldn't be selfish.

"Yes, all right Carlotta. Are you ready for it?"

"Oh yes, uncle Luigi, I'm very ready."

Roger moved back so that Desley could roll back over and when she did so, he couldn't resist pushing his face into her vagina and giving her another orgasm. Then he pulled out and waved his penis at her.

"Here, Carlotta, here is a present for being such a good girl."

Desley took hold of Roger's cock and pulled it up to her mouth and began to suck him off.

The two gazed into each others eyes, contentedly knowing that these two adults had enjoyed a fantasy together and that it could quite likely happen again.

The beautiful Desley took her time sucking Roger's cock, making the most of it while it was on offer. Then she stared up at him and made him explode in her mouth, keeping him there while she savoured his cum.

Roger had enjoyed a number of beautiful backsides during his time in Italy where, after he'd shagged them in his special ways and they had orgasmed, his ladies in black would turn and look at him with their special beautiful smiles and utter the word 'Culo', rolling over on their stomachs and pushing themselves up on their knees and presenting Roger with a perfect view of their naked rear ends – their arses and their loving, fluffy triangles.

Never did he disappoint them and over time and with a sometimes difficult instruction process because of language differences, the ladies educated Roger in the preferred ways of pointing his dagger, or stiletto, when once he'd entered that other special place that women have to offer a man.

It was some weeks later, at the end of a business meeting with Desley late one Sunday afternoon, and when they were discussing many things, Roger had somehow let slip his intense enjoyment of that moment in Desley's backside. To his amazement and pleasure, the delightful woman walked around to him and put her arms around him and kissed him passionately. Then she bent over the end her desk and lifted her skirt. Roger's eyes feasted on her silk covered legs, the suspenders and the black knickers with the lacy trim.

"Pull down my knickers, Roger. I would love you in my arse right now, please. In fact I'd love it if you fucked my arse as often as you liked. Don't forget me. Anytime I'm free I'll be more than happily to bend over and let you in for our mutual pleasure."

Roger and Desley shared their anal enthusiasm, both giving an occasional shudder as each experienced those special feelings that people who know how these things work, can really enjoy.

11

MARIA TELLS MARY

WHEN MARIA ARRIVED at the house, she quickly assured Mary that she wasn't bringing bad news and that there was nothing wrong and that her visit was about things which were good and might help Mary.

"There are women like us, Mary, who just need to make love more often. Actually, I would put the number like us at around seventy-percent of women except many don't know and will probably never know what ails them.

"Staying healthy and happy demands that we live our lives fully and without too many restraints. I'm here because I believe I can offer you a solution, an answer to a horny woman's every fantasy."

Mary giggled and topped up Maria's coffee cup.

"Forgive me, Maria but you do sound as though you've taken on the local Tuppa Ware agency. Should I be worried?"

Maria laughed. "Now that you mention, I do, don't I? But no, I'm here to tell you a story and you can tell me when I've finished, what you think. It will take a little while to tell, so please bear with me. But do interrupt at any time if you have a question.

Without saying where it was, Maria began to tell Mary about The Club.

"Imagine a place that is super safe, clean and well run and comfortable, where women can go to interact with men or women in order to enjoy a wide range of mutually agreed upon sexual exploits. I'm here to tell you that there is now such a place and I want to tell you about it.

Over the next forty minutes, Maria provided details of the organisation of The Club and the required code of behaviour. She thought it best to begin with what happens at the club because that was really what people want to know most and what Mary would be most interested in asking questions about.

And ask questions, she did.

By the time Maria had completed her discourse, Mary was truly excited. Maria asked her to repeat some of the things she'd said just to be sure that she had understood the main points.

"So, Maria. I go to The Club and I'm wanting to meet a man, or as you've pointed out, maybe more than one man. I find a seat anywhere in rows six or seven, and settle back to watch the movie.

After just a short wait, a man will come and sit beside me and after a few minutes he will attempt to touch me, most likely on a leg or a breast or an arm. Then its up to me how I respond, encouraging him or discouraging him. If you want to make him work for his grope, refuse him a couple of times, three max, otherwise he will assume your not up for it. To get of rid of him, four rebuttals should do or just keep moving his hand away.

Meanwhile a second or even a third man might turn up and suddenly I've got more than I can safely handle."

Maria laughed at Mary's childlike enthusiasm.

"You've got it Mary."

"If I'm not getting any takers in sex or seven, I can go and pick a shy bloke from rows four or five and do whatever I like with him.

"And if I want to meet up with a woman, I go and sit in rows eight and nine. In those rows we approach each other with signals - smiles and hand gestures. Sensitive touching and groping, and kissing and licking coming a few minutes later.

And if I'm with someone and we don't want to be interrupted by another horny person, we sit in rows ten, eleven or twelve. We also sit in those rows if we simply want to be alone and watch the movie and play with ourselves.

And finally, if I want to get ravaged, I go and park myself in row three where, in just a few moments I will be deluged with gropers and cock wavers prancing around in front and behind me.

The two woman laughed and Maria commented that she would love to make a movie of Mary on her first visits and how it could be hilarious.

"Now do you remember what other stuff is on offer, Mary?"

"Yep! Haven't forgotten a thing. The Gals Only room is where you can go with girlfriends to canoodle more comfortably, and you will also find dildo's there in two sizes. You can also have a wee and powder your nose. You can even use it as a bolt hole to escape from over zealous blokes.

"The Parlour is like the Gals Only room but it caters for both sex couples.

"Lastly, Home Deliveries sounds like the stand out! The sin-bin. Girls can make a booking and say how many blokes they would like to entertain. Allowable numbers are two, three and four."

"How am I doing, Maria, and where the bloody hell can I find this place?"

"Just tell me a couple of the rules Mary. I need to know that you know the rules."

"Easy, Maria, and number one, don't give anyone your name, phone number or address or any information that will allow them to find you anywhere other than at The Club.

"Arrive at The Club clean and properly clothed. I guess that means not covered in shit, and naked.

"Oh yes, important! Avoid getting into conversations. Talking is anathema to fulfilling your lustful desires. We all remember the visual hunk on sporting TV who made the mistake of trying to talk? And the same goes for women."

"So, my love. Just one more question. Would you like to come along as my guest next Tuesday afternoon. If you enjoy it, I'm allowed three visitor passes a year so that you can come with me again. So Mary? Are you game? Can you face all those horny men and women?"

Mary's face became very serious as she murmured, "Yes please Maria. I would love that."

MARY GOES CLUBBING

MARY'S HAD a lot of trouble accepting that The Club was within walking distance of her house. This seemed so ridiculous as to bring Maria's whole story into question. It wasn't until she was safely in the door and facing the wonderful Alvie, as she attached her visitor number, that Mary begin to think the story was true.

"There you go love. Come back and see me if you have any problems."

"I told you how I would be meeting a girlfriend here didn't I? Veronica and I have known each other for years and we work together sometimes. She and I usually sit in rows eight or nine, mainly to meet girls, but occasionally we hook up with a bloke or two. And if we are fishing for a man, we'll move back a couple of rows. You can sit with us while you're settling in and then wander off to explore and see the sights. You might be shocked."

Mary looked around, wide-eyed.

"It is so beautifully designed, isn't it."

"Wait until you've seen the cinema, Mary. That is the centre of this world."

Veronica called out as she arrived through the front door and the two waited for her to join them. Maria introduced them.

"I've already filled Veronica in on who you are Mary. She said she was excited for you and wished it was her first time. But that is what we always say about anything, isn't it."

The three entered the dimly lit cinema and Maria pointed out that Mary's eyes would soon adjust so that she would be able to see everything going on around her, to which Veronica responded with, "but she really only wants to see the hot bits, like the rest of us."

Tuesday was just another normal day at The Club and as with every other day, activity hotted up a bit an hour or so after The Club opened.

Maria and Veronica stood each side of Mary and each took a hand so that she didn't fall down.

"A lot of people in heels topple over in the isles because of the steep slope and the dim lighting."

Mary suddenly found herself staring down at the movie screen watching as a woman attempted to swallow a very large penis while making sucking noises. She wanted to keep watching but her friends wanted to move her on.

"You said I could just come and sit in the front row and watch the movie, didn't you, Maria?"

"Yes, darling, but surely you wouldn't deny all the other people access to your delightful self. What a waste of a body that would be."

"She will probably never look at the screen again, once she gets active, don't you think, Veronica?"

Mary suddenly stopped in her tracks. "Oh my God, I've just noticed something."

Maria and Veronica laughed and Veronica said, "Well thank God for that. And do you like what you are seeing, Mary?"

Maria and Veronica smiled at each other in the dim light and glanced over to where Mary was staring. A few seats up and across the other side of the next isle, a woman was on her knees on her seat and a man behind her had just pulled down her panties and was feeling between her legs. In front of the woman, another man was holding out his erection towards her face as an offering.

Mary gazed at the scene in silence. She was mesmerised.

Maria noticed a woman heading slowly up towards the threesome.

"Mary? Just watch that woman approaching the people who you are looking at. She is coming towards them from the other side of the row. I think she's moving in to try and get some of the action."

Mary looked and gasped. "My God you're right. Look! She's got her hands on the cock of the man at the back and she's helping him put it into the lady without knickers. And look, another man is arriving and he's pulling up the dress of the woman who has just arrived. This is incredible."

Veronica giggled, "They must be early starters. There's not usually that much action until a bit later.

Maria agreed, "She is obviously a morning person."

"Welcome to The Club, Mary. Veronica and I hope you will enjoy yourself."

Maria and Veronica looked at each other and smiled. Then they moved as one, leading Mary to a seat in row seven and each took a seat on either side of her. Then Veronica turned and smiled at Mary and reached down and lifted Mary's skirt and stared excitedly at her substantial blue stockinged legs while Maria unbuttoned Mary's top, releasing her huge bust. Then Maria pulled down the bra straps and eased two big beautiful bosoms from their cups and rubbed her fingers on a nipple.

Veronica reached under Mary's backside and found the top of her knickers and slowly pulled them down and over her knees while Maria licked and kissed Mary's massive breasts.

Mary had initially made noises of protest, but not for long. She had wanted to watch the couple up further, but she realised that what she had here was much better.

Veronica began to kiss Mary on the lips while gently caressing her large bare thighs above her stockings and this quickly turned into a passionate exchange. Mary turned and embraced Veronica around the shoulders and wanted to completely devour the small woman. Veronica responded and took Mary's hand and guided it up under her short skirt and whispered to Mary, "Please feel me up, Mary. Finger me you beautiful woman."

This first time with the girls was getting Mary's juices running as they hadn't for a very long time. It suddenly reminded her of Helen's seduction of her the year before. It felt almost similarly religious which sounded silly. But having her hands busily discovering the small delicate woman's special places was amazing.

"Oh Veronica, you little darling. I just want to fuck your beautiful little pussy."

Maria likewise dragged Mary's other hand up under her skirt and pressed her fingers to her vagina. But then the women were suddenly interrupted.

Another woman joined them and was kissing Maria while removing her own top and exposing her bosom. Maria responded quickly, dragging the stranger's top off and then sucking her breasts. Moments later, a man arrived and touched both women's breasts while his erection stood waving in the air.

The newly arrived woman stopped and looked at it then took hold of it and sucked it briefly before looking around at everyone before asking if any of them needed a cock in their cunt.

To Mary's surprise, Veronica called out. "Yes please. Come around to this side and I'll have it, thanks."

Veronica turned and looked lovingly at Mary.

"You've made my pussy feel really good Mary so I'll have some cock to go with it. I can usually come in a very short time when I get fucked. You will enjoy it too, my love. I'll make sure of that.

The man made his way around to the other side and parked himself next to Veronica.

"Mary, darling. Will you give him a suck and a rub and make him wet while I position myself to climb onto him."

Mary did as she was asked, reaching her head down and taking hold of the gentleman's quite large cock. She lovingly tugged at it then she leant over and put her mouth over it and slurped saliva on him.

Moments later, Veronica lifted herself up and impaled the man's member in her tiny pussy. Then she jiggled up and down energetically and in no time, she gurgled and moaned and twitched and came. Then she removed him and suddenly she was back kissing Mary like she'd never left.

It all happened so quickly and Mary found that she had loved the whole event, so much so that she was now totally in love with the doll-like Veronica.

The man disappeared and then Mary heard Maria scream and looked down to see her thrusting her cunt hard agains the mouth of the unknown woman and it seemed that the woman was coming at the same time and just a few moments later the two were enjoying celebratory kissing. Mary heard Maria whisper, "Thank you", and the woman replying "my pleasure". Then the visitor was gone.

Maria reached across Mary and slipped a hand into Veronica's tiny bra.

"I love you two horny bitches. You are the best!"

If Mary thought the party was over, she was wrong.

"I need a pee," announced Veronica as she adjusted her clothing.

"I'm taking Mary to the Gals Room. We'll take a booth and relax. We so want to eat each other out, don't we my darling?" Veronica looked lovingly at Mary.

"Hope that's okay with you Maria. I'll catch you tomorrow if you're not here when we come out."

Maria looked at Mary and reached out and took her hand and smiled wickedly.

"You might be about to have the best moments of your visit, Mary. Just do whatever Veronica tells you and enjoy yourself."

Veronica led the way back up the aisle, walking slowly so that Mary could look around at what other folk were up to. Mary was still partly dazed from recent events plus she was excitedly attempting to foresee her upcoming moments with Veronica.

Mary was torn between staring at the beautiful apparition of Veronica's perfect little body swaying from side to side in front of her, and perving on the club members activities on either side.

For her benefit, Veronica would stop when she thought Mary might be interested to gaze on a particular exchange of sexual favours happening close by.

Each time she did this, she would kiss Mary on her cheek and fondle her buttocks and nod her head towards what she had noticed and while Mary watched with fascination as one woman helped another by dragging a cock she was sucking, over to perform in between her friends legs, Veronica continued to run a hand over Mary's posterior. And when Mary stared at a woman who was pretending to be oblivious to the fact that her naked breasts were being gently groped by a man sitting behind her, Veronica nibbled Mary's ear and whispered endearing messages, telling her what she wanted Mary to do to her once they were alone.

As the two neared the top of the aisle, Veronica stopped and nodded towards what was happening in the notorious row three, known to some as The Jungle and to others as Gang-bang Alley.

"This is where you come for something fast and furious, Mary. Maria occasionally likes to park herself there but I make her do it without me. I'm not against it and I would like to try it one day, but not yet. I think it's because I'm so small and I'm frightened it might be too rough. Besides, there are more than enough nice and more gentle things to do here."

Mary's mouth dropped and she whispered, "Oh my God!", staring at what was happening in row three.

Two near naked women were kneeling on their seats, side by side and with their rear ends thrust upwards and slowly wriggling to entice the half-a-dozen men who stood behind them taking turns filling their cunts and arses. The womens heads were resting on the backs of the seats and their mouths were being fed by a platoon of penises. As one cock was being sucked, the woman's hands would be tugging on two others.

Every so often one of the two women would scream loudly and it would rise above the hubbub of the cinema.

"I'd guess that those two are friends and they came here either as a dare or to celebrate something; a divorce maybe. Row three doesn't get a lot of visitors so your quite privileged to see this rare event."

Mary was dumfounded and deep down, she was sexually aroused by what she was watching.

Then Veronica turned Mary's head and kissed her.

"Come along darling. The Gals Room is just here. I want you."

VERONICA MAKES A MOVE

WHILE VERONICA WENT into the toilet for a pee, Mary surveyed the Gals Only room. It was tastefully furnished with a low table, arm chairs and two sofa's. A huge vase of fresh flowers adorned the table and jugs of water and glasses sat on a side cupboard and etchings of erotic artworks hung on the walls. There were six doors which opened on to private booths and four were ajar and when Mary peeped into one, she could see that these too, had vases of flowers and water jugs and artworks on the walls as well as two armchairs and a bed on which lay pillows and bolsters.

Mary could hear happy giggles and squeals and moaning coming from the two booths where the doors were closed. One door showed a red engaged sign but the second showed green meaning it wasn't locked. The other difference was that the first had the curtains pulled completely across but the windows on the second occupied booth were only partly closed, allowing anyone to peep in.

Veronica later told Mary that partly drawn curtains and a green door sign signalled that the occupants would be happy to receive visitors.

Mary would have liked to peep but then Veronica re-appeared and took Mary's hand and led her to a booth and they went in. She locked the door and pulled across the curtains then turned and took Mary in her arms and reached up on her toes and the two kissed.

Both women were excited to be alone together and Mary nervously watched as Veronica dropped her skirt to the floor and stepped out of it, displaying her perfect little body. Mary stared at this most youthful looking fifty-something year-old and a part of her cried out, wanting to devour Veronica or even to be Veronica, standing there in her red stockings and suspender belt and red stilettos and her naughty little red bra that only just reached above her nipples. Veronica's straight black bobbed hair framed her beautiful face and accentuated the wide always open smiling mouth and big cupid lips and emphasised the tiny doll's big angelic brown eyes.

Veronica bent down and lifted the hem of Mary's dress, lifting it up and over her head and dropping it on a chair nearby. Then she stood back and stared at the full-bodied Mary in her blue lace-up bodice corselet and her blue stockings and high heels.

Mary stood still for Veronica's slow inspection. First the woman put her fingers on the white flesh just above Mary's stockings. She seemed intent on the spot where Mary's thigh bulged slightly above the patterned stocking top where the suspender curved around.

Then Veronica lifted Mary's left arm and pushed her face into her armpit and inhaled. Then she licked just below the arm before moving her face to be in front of Mary's breasts.

Veronica small stature meant that, in her high heels, her face was inline with Mary's chest. She lifted one hand and her fingers took hold of and fondled a nipple.

Then she took Mary's hand and led her to the bed.

The two hugged and kissed. Both loved kissing and agreed that proper passionate kissing was the key to making love.

"Mary, my sweet darling, I must tell you first that I am blessed with that rare ability to cum pretty much whenever I want to. Right now I really want to sit on your face and cum on your mouth. Can I do that, please? And Mary, I want you to treat me like your sex doll. Anything you want is all right by me. Don't hold back. Let us be lovers to the full. I desperately want to cum all over you."

Mary listened to what Veronica said and joyfully stared at the petite doll-like sex toy nestled in her arms and mentally drooled as she considered just a few of the things she could imagine doing to Veronica.

And, almost as if Veronica had read Mary's mind, the sex doll spoke in a quiet and reassuring voice.

"Oh yes, I forgot to mention that there are sex toys in that draw, dildos large and small. And yes, Mary my love I intend to use them on you and would love you to use them with me. Feel free to shag me with them and send me to heaven, Mary. And it might surprise you, but even my tiny bottom will welcome your attention.

"And Mary, you will be my sex doll to love and to hold.

It wasn't long before Veronica lifted herself up and swung a leg over Mary's chest. She looked down at Mary lovingly as she moved her perfect little bottom backwards and forwards and side to side over Mary's large bosom. Then she put Mary's arms down beside her and moved up and hovered her little vagina over Mary's mouth. Mary gasped and felt a quiver in her groin.

"Now, my darling. I can cum quickly or slowly and right now I think I want to come slowly. I'm going to rub my wet pussy all over your face. You can lick me and push your tongue or nose into me and when I decide to orgasm, I'll tell my sex slave so that she can grasp me tight and hold me. I would love that."

End

14

ROGER AND HELEN

IT WAS a week or so after Rosa's birthday and it was after dinner one night, that Frederico dropped a booklet on the coffee table in the lounge and asked Helen if she knew about The Club.

"No, darling, I've no idea what you are talking about my love. Should I know? Are we going to be selling raffle tickets for it?"

Freddy laughed. He had spent the afternoon with Roger and Bertie at their fortnightly coffee and cake session upstairs at the Ampersand Cafe in Paddington.

"Roger told us all about it today. He was employed to write up and design this booklet for the owner. I must say that I was shocked when I heard about it, especially when I found out where it was located. I'm still a bit shocked but I'm starting to sort it out in my head."

Helen looked at her husband quizzically, "What on earth are you taking about, darling. Not much shocks you. The last time was when you discovered you were going to be a father for the second time in a month. Should I be worried?"

Freddy spent the next thirty minutes filling Helen in on what he knew about The Club. While he did this, she inspected the booklet he'd brought home.

"I suppose the biggest shock is that it's all happening just down the road," Freddy said.

Helen was intrigued that such a thing existed and begged her husband for more details and asking questions that he didn't have answers for such as "Did husbands and wives go together sometimes or did they just meet up accidentally at The Club?"

They talked about The Club for the rest of the evening. Freddy related and often repeating all that Roger had told him and said how Bertie had mentioned that he and Rosa knew Desley, the owner and her brother Arnold quite well and that he had also met her mother, who was instrumental in getting Eros Crescent renamed. He said she was a fine woman and he wished her well.

Helen, as did Freddy, had more questions than she or he could possibly think up answers for. But as the night drew on and Freddy opened a second bottle of red wine, the two began to see the funny side of things and make jokes.

"Well, darling. I think we should join and then I will put on a wig and enjoy pretending to be somebody else and letting you seduce me, thinking I was the woman in the next street you've always had the hots for."

Freddy giggled.

"I wonder if she is a member?"

Helen punched him but missed and he caught her in his arms and kissed her.

"I suppose membership would fit into our sharing and caring philosophy. What do you think? I guess it's a matter of how much caring and how much sharing we are prepared to get involved in. As you know, darling. In matters of where one expends energy, I'm a bit stretched at the moment," Freddy managed to say with only the slightest hint of an alcohol inspired slur.

Freddy looked at Helen intently, searching for clues of how she thought about it, knowing full well that she was uneasy about him spending so much time with Freya and Sophie.

Helen smiled at her lovely husband and chose her words carefully.

"Well, I seem to have a lot of time on my hands lately Freddy. My lovers all seem to be pregnant or otherwise engaged. Even Mary is making excuses not to see me and Polly is about to be raced off by a young aristocratic polo-playing lad from the Hunter Vally.

"In truth, my love, I do have a small space in my daily routine for a caring and sharing dalliance. But if we joined, it should be as a couple, don't you think. You might just need an occasional change of scenery? I think the daddy-to-be deserves that. We would need to coordinate our club activities so as not to clash, of course."

Freddy leant back on the sofa and smiled at his true love.

"You know that you will always be the most important woman in my life, Helen. I am sorry if you are going through a difficult period with everyone, including me. I'm not against you joining The Club and if they have a special rate for couples, I'm happy to become a member."

There was a silence as the two considered the situation.

"I'll check it out darling."

"Oh yes, Helen. I forgot to mention that we have to be nominated by an existing member. I suspect Roger can help us there. Check with him first."

It was coincidental that Helen phoned Roger about the club as he and Caroline were talking about it. Helen told him that Freddy had shown her the booklet and they had talked about joining The Club.

"He suggested I call you, Roger. He thought you might be able to take me there as a guest. Is that possible? Would you mind?"

Roger was a little surprised to receive Helen's request, but he told her that he wold be happy to show her around and would tomorrow, Wednesday, at 2 o'clock be okay? Helen said that it would be a good time and then she asked him how Caroline had responded to the subject of The Club and Roger was able to say that the two of them were discussing it when she called.

"Well, I'd better leave you to it. Love to Caroline. Tell her that we will have much to talk about when I see her after our adventure."

Caroline had heard all that Helen had said and was much amused.

"Well, Roger. I'm only away for a short time and you have

successfully impregnated someone, shagged the home help, and written a manifesto which could revolutionise western culture as we know it. A girl has to be impressed. Now! When do I get to go to The Club?"

Roger quickly thought about it and replied, "Tomorrow at 2 o'clock be okay with you? You and Helen can share the experience."

Helen and Catherine were excited to see each other and hugged and kissed.

Roger opened The Club door and ushered his lovely ladies into the foyer. Alvie looked up and smiled and Roger introduced her to his two accomplices.

"So good to see you, Roger. I see you've brought your own ladies. Aren't those you meet here good enough for you?"

Everyone laughed and Caroline suggested that now she was back, she would expect that Alvie might see less of him. Alvie went along with the ruse and said how Roger was rather particular and now, having met Caroline, she understood why.

Caroline thanked her and confessed that because she was now pregnant, Alvie might see him more frequently over the coming months.

Roger acted the tourist guide part perfectly, fielding question after question. Even though he had and Freddy had explained much to their partners, as so often happens, things don't sink in so that they both asked how many men could be entertained in the Home Delivery rooms, and both asked him to explain the twelve rows of seating and their designations to better understand how one learnt to shop for whatever it was you were looking for.

Going inside the theatre was the most exciting moment for both of them.

As Roger walked them slowly down the side aisle and their eyes grew accustomed to the reduced light, both Caroline and Helen would touch each other to draw attention to something. Then they watched in awe as a man pushed down the bra on the woman in the seat in front of him and gently levered her breasts out, one at a time before fondling them.

"My God, Caroline. Imagine this on daytime TV."

Just moments later they were looking at a woman who was staring at the movie screen and seemingly absorbed in the movie. She wore a top coat which was pulled back and exposing her naked breasts, suggesting that the coat was her only piece of clothing. On either side sat a man each with his hand on one of her breasts. But of greater note was the fact that both men's cocks were exposed and erect and being slowly rubbed by the woman in the coat.

"Astonishing! And I thought I'd seen it all. My God. No woman need want for anything every again," said Caroline, holding Helen's hand for reassurance.

When they eventually managed to get further down, the two gasped in unison as they saw two women cuddling each each other in row eight while blatantly exposing themselves to the world.

That was when Helen and Caroline both exclaimed as one, that they wanted to try rows eight or nine to see if they could get some attention.

Roger looked and listened and laughed and then realised that the two were being serious.

"Why don't I leave you here for a little while then? Even if you don't get any takers, you will at least be able to relax and feel the vibes of the place and understand it all a bit better.

Helen and Caroline looked at each other and smiled. Then they told Roger that they thought that this was a good idea. And as they hadn't had any time alone together since Caroline's return, this would be as good a place as any for them to start.

Roger smiled at the two beauties, and said how he would try to find something to do for the next half-hour or so, to which Caroline replied, that she thought she had seen an attractive woman arriving in row six and maybe he should check her out.

Roger turned to retrace his steps and rejoiced that Caroline and Helen had so readily settled into the idea of The Club.

Roger returned and as he approached row eight, he realised that his visitors had indeed attracted their own visitors. It looked as though the couple who were already there when Caroline and Helen arrived, had moved over to join them.

Helen was on her knees with her head buried between the legs of a woman who was bare breasted. The other woman was between Caroline's legs, moving her head rhythmically up and down. Caroline's breasts were also uncovered and each of the sitting woman had a hand on the others breast. It was indeed a restful but exciting scene and Roger didn't want to interrupt it.

Roger met Caroline and Helen as they were slowly making their way up the aisle from where they had been sitting. They were stopping regularly to look at what was going on and when Roger approached, they were silently witnessing an event in row three, The Jungle.

"Oh my God! How many men has she got behind her now?"

"I think it must be four plus the one laying on the seat under her. He's already made his entrance, from what I can see, so I can only guess where the others might be putting theirs."

Roger stood and watched unnoticed as his two companions stared at what was usually a once-a-day event, if that. He thought how good it was that they had seen so much on their first visit.

"We would like to come back here. Helen and I enjoyed ourselves very much, didn't we Helen?"

Then Roger quipped, "Anyone for a cup of tea or coffee?"

"Oh yes. I've tried to call Helen in case she wanted to come but there was no answer. If she comes by looking for me, tell her I'm sorry I missed her but I'll be back at around three or four o'clock."

Then Caroline gave Roger an odd look.

"You might not have noticed but Helen and Frederico are going through a bit of a thing, partly because of Sofi and Freya's wanting to see more of Freddy now they are going to have his babies.

"We talked about it and she said she hoped this jealousy thing she was feeling wasn't going to happen with me and Alice.

"I told her that so far, Alice hasn't acted in any way that seemed remotely possessive. I also said that if she did, it might be different for us because she and I are closer in age than Helen and the two girls.

"I'm mentioning it so that if she shows up, you won't be too blokesy. Bye darling!"

Caroline turned back to look at Roger. She was very relaxed, but offered him an odd look and then smiled.

"Come to think of it, Roger, if she does happen to call in, I'm certain that it would be much appreciated by her and me if you were able to be especially nice to her, seeing how lonely she's feeling. You get my drift, don't you darling. Just a last minuted thought. See you later in the day, sweetheart. I'll try to think of something special to bring home."

Caroline blew Roger a kiss and disappeared.

Roger had just returned to his desk with his cup of coffee when there was a knock at the door and Helen's voice called out.

"Can I come in?"

Roger heard the door close.

"I'm in here, Helen. Come through."

Helen appeared at the door of his office come spare bedroom.

"Hi Roger. It's so lovely and warm in here. Is the girl around?"

Roger looked up and was immediately smitten yet again with the beautiful wife of his best friend, Frederico. This mature woman ticked more of his boxes than he ever thought possible.

A smiling Helen stood in the doorway dressed in a heavy jumper under a see-through poncho. He noticed her tweed skirt and heavy brown stockings and practical brown walking shoes. Her medium length brown hair had been messed up by the violent winds blowing outside.

"You've missed the girls. They've gone of to do pampering or some such thing that men don't really understand. Caroline told me to pass on that she had tried to contact you but without success."

Helen stared at Roger as though trying to read his inner thoughts.

"Never mind. I'll go and put the heater on in my studio and try to get creative. Looks like you are pretty busy, Roger, so I won't interrupt you."

Roger's response was very quick.

"I'd love you to stay, Helen, that's if you would like to. I'm just going through stuff that Desley gave me. She wants me to comment on the things people have left in the suggestion boxes at the club and report back with my thoughts. It could be fun. You might help me, perhaps.

"After that, I'm about to restart a major project for her that stopped because of lockdown, but I'm putting that off for a couple of days until I get more information.

"Please stay. It's warm here and there are comfy chairs and even a bed if you get tired and need to take a snooze. And I will even attempt to make you a perfect coffee if you so desire."

Roger was aware that he was selfishly wanting Helen to be here with him while at the same time, attempting to fulfil Carolin's wish that he be especially nice to her girl friend.

Helen's stare softened and she agreed that his office was probably the right place to be given how cold and windy it was outside.

Helen came in and walked over to the armchair at the end of Roger's desk, and made herself comfortable, laying her arms on the soft chair arms and crossing her legs.

"Have you and Caroline sorted out your wedding arrangements, Roger? The last time I saw the two of you together, she was telling you to sod off. I get the feeling that that is well behind you now."

Roger's face made a tight lipped grimace.

"A man never really know where he stands with a woman. But to answer your question, yes, I think our betrothal will happen in the spring, complete with a full lesbian ceremony and service.

"I suspect I'll be the only man there. Oh, no. Freddy will have to be best man of course. I haven't asked him yet. I hope he'll be up for it."

Helen seemed to stiffen in her chair.

"You might like to consider a plan B, Roger. Freddy is preoccupied with his other wives to the point of not having time for anything else."

Roger reminded himself that Caroline had told him that Helen was in a difficult space at the moment. He looked at Helen and smiled.

"Thank you Helen. I'll remember that."

He removed the two clips holding the mens and womens notes from the suggestion boxes at The Club.

"Okay, Helen. Are you ready? I'm going to start by just reading quickly through all of them, then we can go back and address each question in detail.

"Lets start with the women's suggestions."

15

SUGGESTION BOX RESULTS

HELEN HAD RESPONDED to the humour of the moment and laughed loudly which encouraged Roger to think that she was likely to relax and enjoy her visit and maybe his company.

Helen got up and came over and stood beside Roger enthusiastically urging him to let her see, what the girls have to say.

"From the ladies suggestions box, we have;

"Note one: Do condoms get recycled and if so what do they end up as? Signed: Sticky-fingers.

"Note two: Could we please have deodorant available for sale at the kiosk, particularly men's deodorant? Signed: Nosegay Gertie

"Note three: Could we have a service via the smart card where a woman can book a man for a long session of cock sucking. Men generally are in too much of a hurry to move on to the next bit. Signed: The Pointer Sisters

"That sounds reasonable," Roger mumbled.

"Note four: One man and one woman for extended anal sex sessions in private. Signed: Bottom Draw

"Oh wow! How do I find this woman? My fantasy could be fulfilled after all these years."

Roger heard Helen gasp and looked up at her. Helen was staring at the last entry and then she looked at Roger. She seemed as though she was trying to sort something out in her head. Then she reached down and took Roger's hand in hers and looked at him strangely.

"Is everything all right, Helen?

Roger held onto her hand and looked up at her, waiting for her response.

"I wrote that last one, Roger. I went for a pee just before we left The Club the other day and just couldn't resist adding a suggestion."

The two stared at each other as though they were about to go through a door to an unknown land.

Roger found himself reaching out with his other hand to Helen's leg standing beside his chair. He touched her on her calf and felt the excitement of gently rubbing her stocking covered leg.

Helen let go of Roger's hand and touched his face and looked longingly at him.

"Is that suggestion really what you would like, Helen."

"Oh yes Roger. Oh yes, it really is."

Helen clasped the sitting Roger's head to her bosom as Roger's hand moved slowly up her leg. He didn't want to frighten her or for her to think he was just making out for the sake of it.

"Roger?"

"Yes, Helen?"

"If it is true that we both want the same thing, then I should tell you that at the moment, no matter what I want, I'm feeling quite fragile and vulnerable and could find it difficult to respond to you in the way we both would want. One thing that would help me would be for you to just kiss me, Roger.

"Stand up and kiss me please Roger. I need to sort out my emotions and kissing will do it for me."

Roger stood up and put his arms around Helen, feeling her collapse into him. Then he felt her trembling and heard her sobbing and he pulled her closer. She lifted her head and her eyes shone and she put her mouth on his and the two melted into one another.

After trembling for some time whilst still managing to kiss Roger, Helen moved her head back so that she could look at him.

"I must warn you that I won't be able to stop once we start, Roger.

Once I give you my rear you will have me forever. I will want you there and you will want to be there, be it for just ten minutes or for hours on end. If you can give me what I crave then you will never get rid of me."

Helen felt Roger's cock growing in his pants against her belly and she relaxed and smiled and went back to kissing him.

Roger ventured to put a hand down over Helen's thick skirt and massage her backside. Then he lifted her big woollen sweater up to her neck and looked down at her beautiful chest, slowly heaving with emotion. Helen breathed deeply and he noticed she'd stopped trembling. She reached up and moved his head so that she could put her lips back on his and they tongued each other.

"I'm ready, Roger," Helen whispered. "Before you take me anally you will have to fuck me a little bit. It will get things wet for me and I so love to be wet."

Roger heard what Helen said. He didn't want to let her go but he knew he would have to. He wanted what she wanted and they both wanted it now.

Roger reached behind Helen and unzipped her skirt and it fell to the floor. Then Roger held her hand while he stood back to look at her. She was a vision splendid. He turned her around and looked at her backside. Roger was looking at his ideal woman.

Roger knew that he wanted to move on with Helen. He unzipped his pants and removed them along with his boxer shorts and his member stood up tall and straight and Helen stared at it.

"I'm feeling better every moment, Roger. And I can see you are serious. Take off my undies and inspect and touch my rear, Roger. I'm desperate for you to feel me."

Helen reached out and took hold of Roger's cock and whispered to it.

"You are going to heaven and taking me with you. You will become mine and I will become yours."

Helen looked deep into Roger's eyes then she slipped a hand into her knickers and rubbed herself.

"My activities in recent years have only been with women, Roger. This feels very much like my first time and I'm nervous.

"Women accept other womens bodies and behaviour quite easily. So if I tell you that I have a very hairy vagina and that I often make a lot of noise during sex and I sometimes bite people, will that put you off me? Before I can relax, I need to feel secure, Roger. Help me feel secure, you lovely man."

Roger stepped back a little and looked down at Helen's beautiful body. He stared at her strong stockinged legs then with one hand he pushed down Helen's knickers to her knees and uncovered her hairy crotch and with the other he felt her between the legs, bunching her ample bush in his palm.

"How beautiful you are, Helen. And I love your hairy pussy. You know that I've had two years in Italy where hair down here is worshipped, so believe me when I say I will happily worship you. And I should confess that I can be noisey too."

Helen gave a little start and Roger felt her hand grasp him more tightly, and his cock jumped in appreciation.

Helen put her other hand up to his head and pulled his face to hers and opened her mouth and engulfed Roger's lips, then pushed her tongue into him. As she did so she let go of his member and reached down and removed her panties.

"Fuck my bushy cunt first, please Roger. Then you may take my other spot. I want you to fuck it for ever."

Roger moved Helen over to the bed and lowered her, all without letting go of her sweet spot. Then he pushed her legs apart and removed her hand and nestled the end of his prick in her now very wet hairy vagina, and slowly moved it right in. Helen orgasmed immediately murmuring "Already? Oh God!"

The two bodies clasped each other tightly and tongued each other and Helen's body shook regularly with tiny orgasms that she was prone to when excitement overwhelmed her, and which she hadn't experienced for a very long time.

Helen removed her mouth from Roger's. "Oh Roger, this might end up killing me. This is so beautiful I will never want it to end. Spoil me more Roger and tell me that you love me. I promise I won't hold you to anything you say. Tell me you love me and that you love being in my hairy cunt."

Roger needed little prompting.

"How could I not love you, you beautiful sexy bitch? My cock is in paradise. How will I be able to leave it for that other spot at the back. You will still want me in the back, won't you?"

Helen swung her legs around Roger's waist and pulled him into her, then gave a little laugh.

"Oh Roger. You are such a joy. I want you everywhere all at once. But having you in my arse should settle me down. Take it whenever you wish, my darling. Your cock is nice and wet now and my bum is already screaming out for your attention.

"And Roger. If Caroline comes home and finds us like this, don't worry. She put me up to it. She said she was so fed up with seeing me miserable that she insisted that I have you. I love her so much."

Roger had actually suspected something when Caroline had looked at him as she was leaving and how she had commented that she would like him to be especially nice to Helen. "Well, if she does find us, then she will just have to join in," Roger mused.

Roger slowly removed himself from the hairy heaven. Then he kissed Helen lovingly, and lifted up her legs and backside to make her arse easily accessible.

"I want you this way, Helen. I'll role you over later."

Helen wriggled to position herself in readiness, "Yes, sweetheart. I'm ready. Which ever way is fine."

Roger kissed and licked Helen's anus then inserted two fingers and moved them about. Then with both hands, he opened her hole and stretched it a little and peered inside the pink tunnel. Then he entered her, gently at first and then more assertively.

"Oh God! Yes, yes, yes!"

SETTLING DOWN

HELEN WAS happy and so was Roger. The tunnel felt wonderful on his cock and he knew that he could spend a long time there, quietly moving his dagger or stiletto as his Italian twins had tutored him.

Roger looked down at Helen's smiling face, both rejoicing in their erotic pleasure.

The two shagged on through the early afternoon with intermittent kissing and shouting. The they rested and Roger brought his new love, cake and ginger beer. Then they looked at each other and Helen rolled over onto her knees again and lifted her bum and both nodded indicating it was time for more shagging.

"Oh, Roger, this is so beautiful. I just want you to shag me forever. Your big cock feels so wonderful. I just want to cry."

Suddenly, Helen burst into tears and sobbed, her body shaking in unison with Roger's shagging motions.

Then Caroline walked through the door.

"Oh my God, how beautiful you both look. But why is Helen crying?"

Helen looked around at Caroline and put a hand out towards her and Caroline responded. She dragged her thick jumper off over her head, unbuttoned her blouse and threw herself on the bed beside her female idol. As she did so, Helen orgasmed for the umpteenth time, dragging Caroline to her and raining tears and saliva on Caroline's bosom.

"I'm so happy, Caroline. Thank you so much. I won't let Roger stop. I hope you don't mind. I hadn't realised how much I needed this moment. He has been so wonderful and I can't stop shagging him. Why don't you lie beneath me and share. I could lick you and you could play with me and him. I would so love that."

Caroline kissed Helen energetically.

"Oh, my dearest Helen, yes, please. Let's do that."

Helen pushed her legs apart far enough for Caroline to squeeze between them, then, as Caroline gently fingered Helen's cunt, Helen reciprocated, fastening her mouth on Caroline's wet and fluffy special place.

Caroline put her head to one side so that she could peer up at Roger while at the same time, she took his testicles in her other hand. "Love you darling," she called. Then in a semi jocular voice loud enough for Helen to hear, she called out.

"Fuck the beautiful bitch, you wonderful man. I can feel you, and it feels as though you are fucking me too. I love it!

"I think you two are cock-in-the arse loving sluts. I think Helen will want this at least once a fortnight. Am I right Helen? Don't bother answering. I know I'm right. We'll arrange it."

Then Caroline arched her back and enjoyed a very strong orgasm triggering the same thing in Helen causing her to give way to her final surrender as she collapsed on top of Caroline, and leaving Roger sitting back with a still hungry cock.

"Sorry, Roger."

Caroline seized the opportunity and rolled herself out and around and pulled her lover on top of her and, gripping Roger's cock firmly in one hand, she led him to her own little door to heaven nestled between her buttocks, and fed him in.

"Finish yourself off there please darling, as hard and as soon as you like. You deserve it, sweetheart. Thank you. I love you."

It was only moments later that Roger orgasmed inside his lover who lifted her body to meet him and come with him. And Helen felt it and added a small scream and her body shook violently in unison with her two loves.

So ended Helen's first of many loving moments with Roger.

Helen was excited watching Roger bugger Caroline who had only recently discovered the joys of anal and of course the two would share their orgasms and Roger in the ultimate loving relationship. Helen loved to touch the two of them when they were making love, Caroline's clitoris and Roger's testicles being much favoured along with breasts and buttocks.

Arrangements were made for Helen to come and stay over on those nights when her husband, Frederico was with either of the two pregnant ladies, Sophie and Freya.

Sometimes Helen and Roger would be given space in the afternoon to be alone but often they would invite Caroline along for the ride and the three would shag for a whole afternoon.

And whilst the double bed was fine for three people making love, after a night of excitement, Roger would remove himself and cross the room to sleep in the single bed leaving the two women cuddled up in their post orgasmic slumber.

Who ever woke up first, went and made and delivered a tray of hot drinks then Roger would join the two women and they would all cuddle up and most times they would fall into a second slumber.

As Roger was about to fall into another slumber, a thought flashed through his mind. He saw the club and he saw his recent loves and he understood the meaning of life, but only briefly.

CATCH UP

EROS CRESCENT

No one on Eros Crescent remembers exactly the moment when the words COVID-19 or Corona virus were first uttered in their houses. Needless to say, it would first have been heard on a television report and the importance of the message would have taken a few days to sink in.

The world suddenly changed. Words and phrases like lockdown and self-isolation and social distancing were suddenly in the forefront of all conversations as people enacted the requests of government and the nation to act responsibly to assist in the national objective to achieve what quickly became known as flattening the curve.

For Roger, life couldn't have been less affected. His daily routines required only that he rose from his bed, showered and shaved, ate his breakfast, went for a walk, and made sure he had sufficient pens and paper. Although it did impinge on his new paying project.

He had been asked by Desley to write another booklet similar to the one he'd written for The Club, only this was to be for The Dunking, a venue he had not yet visited or, until now, even heard of.

When Desley explained the concept and related what the setting inside the warehouse was like, Roger was very keen to get started. But the arrival of the virus put an end to that project, at least until further notice.

For Caroline and Jackie and Miranda, staying at home was what they enjoyed anyway, that is when they weren't travelling abroad or window shopping or having coffee in cafe's.

All three women had worked in executive positions in London, but moving overseas brought that era to a close, although they had been invited to join similar companies in Australia.

A top of the range coffee making machine was promptly ordered along with a supply of fair trade East Timorese Maubisse, medium blend. Browsing online shops became the new window shopping.

Instagram took on a new importance as the pandemic took hold around the world. Stories and pictures of people in isolation doing amazing and sometime ridiculous things became the rage. Jackie uploaded hundreds of images of the inside and outside of the house, earning the praise of interior designers and architects.

Helen and her husband Frederico were effected in so far as Freddy's job as a flight controller at the airport was soon to be reduced in the number of hours he worked. However, there was no threat to his income as he was on standby as an essential service. But Helen's work as a freelance Human Resources consultant to industry came to a sudden halt. She embraced online conferencing on Zoom but this was no substitute for real hands-on consulting.

Helen was also restricted in her love life, already reduced as a result of her husbands responsibilities to Helen's two lovers who had inadvertently become pregnant to him.

Sophie and Freya now spent a night a fortnight with Freddy. Unable to visit or have visits from her own lovers, Polly or Celia Ashbee, Helen would just have to manage with her next-door neighbour, Mary. And what looked like the answer to maiden's prayer, The Club had been forced to close.

Mary's only loss of employment was her volunteer job at the Salvation Army Opportunity Shop which she would miss very much. She would also miss her sensual workout with her close friend Janice. But most of all, she would miss her newly found excitement at The Club which she had only recently opened.

Her niece and housemate, Sophie, worked at a horse stud and accepted reduced hours and looked forward to doing baby things at home. Because she and Mary lived next door to Helen and Freddy, the two households would have access to each other when needed. And of course, Freddy was to be the father of Sophie's as yet unborn child.

Alice and Frey both lamented the loss of work in their jobs as school counsellors. They both loved their jobs. Both were pregnant and accepted they would be forced to spend more time at home together.

Like most of the others, they had their favourite sex toys for when they weren't knitting baby clothes or doing jigsaw puzzles. And like so many women in lockdown, they visited female friendly porn sites online. The two decided that they would always share these internet session and happily parked themselves on the sofa, transmitting the websites from their phones to the giant television set via a magic little box. This meant that the images were so big that they felt they were in the same room and this proved most enjoyable on many occasions.

Bertie and Rosa were the older folk who were most vulnerable to the virus. They were happy to be isolated although Bertie complained that he would miss his fortnightly get together for coffee and cake with Freddy and Roger.

Bertie complained that he still had much to say on the subject of breaking down the worlds dependance on the "couples model" as he called it.

"Nothing good will happen while we maintain this ridiculous habit of pairing off for life." Firstly, in over half the cases, it doesn't work and people separated or divorced.

"Secondly, it was obvious that people who stayed in these relationships were deeply frustrated by the repressive demands on them of constantly answering to another person.

"Thirdly, paternity and property ownership where the only reasons this system was maintained and with the likely end of democracy as we know it looming, house prices and pension funds and equity investments were likely to collapse.

"And I haven't even mentioned the problems of religion and religious wars."

Rosa looked at him. She loved him dearly but managed always to call him out.

"You haven't mentioned love once."

"Sex and love are two seperate things, my dear. We both know that."

Most of the close friends and relatives knew that Rosa and Bertie had broken up many years ago and taken lovers. Rosa entered relationships with her close girl friends and occasionally, a man.

Sometime later, she and Bertie got back together as a couple, but both maintained their freedom to embark on other relationships if they so chose, and this arrangement worked very well. It wasn't that they were desperate to take on other romantic adventures, but just knowing that they were free to do so, made the difference. They broke up after almost twenty years and had now been together for nearly fifty years.

"It was a necessary pause," agreed the two of them, lovingly.

The two people that were originally going to be living together but in the end chose not too, were Edith and Jessica. But living at different ends of the same street meant that they would not need to forego their times together. And they, like Maude and the others living in number nineteen, had each other for company if and whenever they wanted.

Edith and Jessica had the boys on hand and could also still get a pizza delivered, although it sometimes took a little longer.

But then they learnt that they would now be sharing the boys with the very sexually active Maude and possibly with the two new girls who moved in to number eleven just before the lock down. Jessica and Edith's plans to invite the new girls in for a pizza, were in hand.

Edith still went for her walk on Mount Eros on most mornings where she usually met her friend Chloe and the two, more than not, would spend loving time together in Chloe's secret cave.

It was thanks to the lockdown, that Jessica met Chloe. Edith had long wanted the two to meet so when was Jessica unable to attend classes she accompanied Edith on her walks.

Jessica and Chloe were instantly friends. Both knew that the other understood Chloe's relationship with Edith. And when the rain fortuitously arrived on their first walk together, all three made haste to the hidden cave and it was only a few minutes before Jessica had Chloe underneath her on the carpet of leaves with Edith dragging first Jessica's then Chloe's shorts and panties off before sitting beside them with her bare breasts available for the occasional grope from both girls.

It was Desley who had the most to lose but she wasn't particularly put out. The Club had to close only two short months after opening and only a few weeks after Desley had formed a partnership with her friend Sally who had opened The Dunking venue. The Dunking was closed too.

Desley welcomed the opportunity to take a rest and review everything about the club and the new venture and be ready to make any necessary changes or recommendations to Sally when they eventually reopened.

She and her partner Alvie, lived on the premises. Alvie knew about Desley's dalliances with Roger who she said she also had a soft spot for.

Desley had laughed, saying that now that they had so much time on their hands, she would endeavour to entice Roger to pop in for a threesome if Alvie didn't mind sharing. To which Alvie replied that she wanted first go.

Maria and her daughter Serina were at first, forced to stay home with grandfather Aldo and the boarder, Giorgio. They mostly worked for older people as cooks and housekeepers in the stately home of Vaucluse and Woollahra.

They successfully applied for positions with the council as carers so that they could continue working.

They both had each other and the two live-in men to play with when they felt like it plus a range of toys they enjoyed.

Maud, the owner of the music school and owner of the property at nineteen Eros Crescent found isolation difficult, severely limiting her adventures although she had managed to entertain herself with young Ashton and Damian after the two became suddenly sexually aware after falling prey to pizza nights with Jessica and Edith.

And Sylvia and Stella, the two girl who she had enjoyed briefly when they stayed over on the night of her house warming party, seducing Maude with the help their bunny outfits, had booked in for music classes and accomodation the week before lockdown. Maud reasoned that maybe life wouldn't be too bad after all.

Peoples attitudes were changed in part by the arrival of the pandemic.

Australia was fortunate that it could close its borders and clamp down easily on travel.

Europe was badly affected and Britain failed in the early stages to take action which might have prevented many of the casualties they suffered.

The USA continued to be the sad case that it had slowly become.

Big enough to make loud noises but also it seemed, too big to be able to maintain good democratic government.

It was presided over by a man who couldn't cope with an enemy he couldn't see and he couldn't lash out at, or verbally deride.

The arrival of the invisible virus was to prove his undoing.

Life on Eros Crescent went on. The residents continued to love each other in many different ways and despite the sudden disruption of the pandemic, there was a feeling of optimism in the air.

Babies were on the way and new life called out for new ideas. And new ideas about how society worked were desperately needed.

Cross your sanitised fingers everyone, and hope.

The three volumes of the Eros Crescent series are available at Amazon Books as paperbacks or Kindle ebooks.

CONTACT

Publisher or review enquiries should include your full name and details in all correspondence.

Email address:
admin@richardlee.biz

RICHARD LEE PUBLISHING

Erotic Fiction

The Eros Crescent trilogy as paperbacks or ebooks:

The Fifi Code

ISBN - 978-0-909431-02-0

Eros Crescent

ISBN - 978-0-909431-05-1

Mount Eros

ISBN - 978-0-909431-08-2

New 2022:

Wet Dreams for Oldies: Never feel lonely again

ISBN: 978-0-909431-22-8

Excerpts from the Eros Crescent series as paperbacks or ebooks:

Janice: A sexual enigma

ISBN - 978-0-909431-10-5

Jessica: A young woman's journey

ISBN - 978-0-909431-13-6

Helen: Enough is not enough

ISBN - 978-0-909431-14-3

Maria: Always available

ISBN - 978-0-909431-15-0

Mary: Catching up

ISBN - 978-0-909431-11-2

The Club: Ladies love it!

ISBN - 978-0-909431-11-2

Happy Honeypots: Swinging in Harmony

ISBN - 978-0-909431-20-4
Roger: Ladies love to pay him
ISBN - 978-0-909431-21-1

Literary Fiction

Australian Short Stories
ISBN - 978-0-909431-00-6

Restless: A novel about two young men growing up
in Australia between 1900 and 1936 (Publication date not set.)

Out of Print Titles

Mathematics for Young Children by Helen Western
ISBN - 978-0-909431-01-3

Currajong: For Those Whom Schools Have Failed
by Bruce Wicking
ISBN - 978-0-909431-03-7

The Puppetry Handbook by Anita Sinclair
ISBN - 978-0-909431-04-4

Wordswork by Chris Davidson & Bruce Wicking
ISBN - 978-0-909431-06-8

Sheep Production by Murray Elliott
ISBN - 978-0-909431-07-5

Ducks for Starters: A Practical Guide to

Backyard Duck Keeping by Bruce Wicking

ISBN - 978-1-875207-00-8

Sweethearts by Colin Talbot

ISBN - 978-1-875207-02-2